YOUNG AT MIDNIGHT

JENNIFER ANN SHORE

Print ISBN: 978-1-7360672-6-0

For Bash,
For the many hours of
your life spent tolerating me
and my music preferences

ONE

I like to think I'm a creature of habit.

Since graduating college, I've spent the better—or worse, depending on how I look at it—part of my twenties cultivating my routine, and I'll be damned if anything's going to throw it off.

There's an art to starting my day, and it begins with a slow and gentle ascent back into consciousness. I usually wake up just before my alarm pings, and I take my time to stretch out my limbs like I'm warming up for the day ahead.

Once I've showered, dressed, straightened my hair, and gathered my belongings, I'm off.

My reverse commute alone is something of an art form, and I'm lucky to be heading into Brooklyn instead of the other way around. Even then, I've learned the hard way that there's a sweet spot in the morning rush, which almost always guarantees me a seat for the ride. It's a little after the earliest risers are off to spin class but before the morning meetings start.

I shove my earbuds in as I head out, grateful that the ride toward my office is long enough to fit in an entire episode of my favorite true crime podcast.

This daily ritual might sound like standard practice—or maybe it's monotonous or boring or all of those things at once—but it's mine.

My job is demanding and can be unpredictable at times, but I'm comforted by the fact that at the very least, my mental and physical spaces are just the way I want them. The tiny studio apartment is just a few blocks from Union Square, a park with buskers, chess players, and the farmers market, which is where I spend most of my weekend mornings.

But today's just a regular Thursday, which means I'm heading my way toward the same building I've gone to nearly every weekday for the past nine years.

Exos's offices are situated at the end of a very trendy neighborhood, and even though I should be desensitized by its location at this point, I exhale contentedly as I take in the stunning views of the East River. Because in a city with millions of people, I like to think I've carved out my own little part of New York.

It's almost comforting to have such order amid the chaos of—

"Watch it!"

I jump in surprise at the demand, then turn to take in the commotion behind me.

As luck would have it, I move just in time to see a random passerby's purse swing to hit the man's coffee cup, but I'm too slow to do anything other than watch in horror as the front of my pristine, white button down is coated by the contents of the nearly full drink.

At least it's an *iced* coffee.

I gasp before stepping aside, out of the flow of foot traffic, to frantically untuck my shirt. The ice and excess liquid splash on the cement at my feet, and I struggle to keep the soaked fabric away from my favorite bra.

"Shit," the guy says, approaching me with his empty cup still in his hand. "I'm so sorry about that."

I smile tightly as I attempt to wring out my shirt onto the sidewalk. "It's fine," I mumble through my irritation. "I'm sure it will come out."

That's a lie.

This shirt was a gift and a very thoughtful splurge after my promotion last year. My mother insisted I needed a "wardrobe worthy of an award-winning *senior* reporter," and now, it's reduced to a weird tie-dye coffee look. The fact that I now reek of mocha and milk is an unwanted addition to the entire scenario.

He clears his throat, and I don't miss the way his eyes linger at the fabric that's nearly transparent.

"Sorry, I don't have any napkins or anything," he says.

"Really, it's fine," I assure him, releasing the bunched-up fabric from my now sticky hands.

"I could buy you a coffee as an apology?"

The last thing I want is to be chatted up by some tech bro as I continue my poor imitation of a wet T-shirt contest.

I have a story due, after all.

"Thanks for the offer," I say lightly as I start walking again. "But I'm going to pass."

"Oh, come on," he argues, appearing at my side.

"No, thank you."

"I know a place right around the corner."

"I really can't," I insist. "I'm already running late."

I pick up my pace and pull my purse in tighter, as if that motion somehow demonstrates how I'm closing myself off from him.

"It's not even nine o'clock yet."

"I'm not interested," I finally snap.

He stops walking, but by the way he huffs, I know I'm not in the clear yet.

"Whatever, bitch," he yells in my direction.

I roll my eyes as I reach the front door of the building, grateful for the security measures of having to scan my badge at the main doors and once again to press the correct floor on the elevator.

The first time I got cursed at by a random stranger on the street, it rattled me to the point of tears, but now, I take it in stride. It's part of the experience of being here—the sign of a true New Yorker is being hardened enough to the point that shit just kind of rolls off your back.

Really, I'm more put-off in how the slight delay knocks my routine out of whack enough that the elevator is more crowded than usual.

My fragrance and appearance draw attention and a few apologetic looks, and I avert my eyes until I arrive at my desk, dropping my bag unceremoniously on top of it.

I drop down to rifle through my bottom drawer, which serves as a catch-all for the random items the *Exos* marketing team has pawned off on me over the years. Pushing aside the stress balls, plastic shot glasses, and pairs of sunglasses, I grab one of the logo shirts folded at the very bottom, and head to the bathroom to change.

When I finally catch my appearance in the mirror, I frown.

Somehow in the scuffle, wisps of my blonde hair came undone from the low ponytail I styled it in this morning, and my lipstick smudged just enough to make me look like I've just rolled out of someone else's bed.

I wish that were the explanation for why I'm so disheveled.

I toss the ruined fabric into the garbage can and try my best to clean my torso with soap and paper towels, but even after I put on the fresh *Exos* merchandise, the smell of coffee lingers.

It's the best I can do, though, and I've spent enough time this morning fretting about my appearance—there are much more important things that need my attention today.

I ignore the feeling of being a little off as I head back to my desk and settle in, turning on my laptop to read my latest piece. It's probably the hundredth time I've read this particular story, but the potential payoff is worth every second of my agonizing over the details and overthinking the quotes I've chosen.

When I graduated from journalism school nearly a decade ago, I was arrogant enough to think I could change the world, and I got a dose of reality pretty quickly.

After slogging along in multiple internships where I was tasked with getting coffee, manually checking over transcriptions, and rarely earning bylines, I met my current boss, Bryan, at an NYU networking event for scholarship students.

At the time, *Exos* was barely considered a news outlet, but with a big investor joining the ownership team and a very determined pair of journalists leading the editorial charge, Bryan left his steady newspaper job to try and shape the publication into something noteworthy.

I barely finished my first drink at the event before he demanded to see my clips, and at some point between drinks two and three, he gave me a verbal job offer.

The next day, I received a more formal one.

And I've been here ever since, steadily rising through the ranks of reporters.

There were growing pains, certainly, but I've stayed away from the lavish parties and workplace drama in favor of my reporting. For the most part, I've been happy with what I've produced, but nothing has come close to what I'm looking at now.

It's the story of a lifetime—well, so far in the lifetime of my career—and I've been chasing it for nearly a year.

I think part of me craves monotony in other aspects of my life because I've had too many ups and downs at my job, like fighting back against online trolls and having sources completely ghost me just before a deadline.

But this story surfaced by chance when I was covering one of the labor union rallies last year. After I finished recording an interview with one of the organizers, he made an offhand comment about his current job not being as bad as working at Ellison Incorporated.

"The hedge fund?" I asked him, jotting down the name in my notes. "What about it is worse?"

He glanced around, ensuring no one paid us any attention. "Look, I've heard this from a friend of a friend, so don't tie my name to it, but you should check into it."

That piqued my interest. "Anything in particular?"

"Employee conditions and some of the financials don't add up from what I hear."

That little tidbit of information sent me on a wonderfully frantic chase for more information.

It didn't take me long to dig into the company's public records and investment details, but it took some time to find enough workers willing to speak on the record about Roger Ellison, the chairman of the board, and the company's rampant discrimination practices.

Not to mention the long list of other violations they need to be held accountable for...

White-collar crime isn't my specialty, necessarily, but there's something about taking down rich, powerful men that thrills me into working super long hours on not-so-great pay.

It's immensely satisfying.

I worked on other stories in the meantime, of course, while setting up interviews and poring over whatever data I could get my hands on. But over time, it became a bit of an obsession to dig into the company's dealings, including some sketchy political connections and more than three blatantly misleading public relations campaigns.

Now, after a year and multiple rounds of editing—not to mention the tedious vetting process by *Exos*'s in-house legal team—we're finally ready to publish it.

I'm glad to get the story out there. I hope it will expose the major wrongdoings of the company, but I think it's just the beginning of what I can do. I want to hold those in power accountable and spur changes into action, both in the private sector and with governmental policy changes.

"What's up, Dakota?" Christina asks, leaning against the edge of my desk.

I blink up at her, somewhat startled at being pulled from my inner monologue. "Nothing."

She quirks an eyebrow at me. "I can tell you're trying to focus on whatever you're doing, but you seem...frazzled. And that's not a description I normally associate with you."

I sigh loudly and sit back. "Some asshole spilled coffee all over me this morning."

"So that's why you look like our employer's biggest fangirl," she says with a smile. "Cute skirt, though."

"Thanks," I deadpan in response to her combination of an insult and a compliment. "But my story is finally getting published tomorrow, so I'm just giving it a few final reads."

"The Ellison one?"

I nod. "Yep."

She shivers. "I hope that scumbag gets thrown in jail. I had to fact-check the quotes from his secretary myself last week and...ugh."

"Don't forget how much money he spent in an attempt to stop workers from unionizing," I remind her. "Which cost—"

"More than the pay increase the workers asked for," she finishes.

I scoff and shake my head. "Awful."

"So, what's your next story? What are you working on when you're finished?"

"I've been pitching an in-depth profile on the woman

8

who chained herself to the UN gates as a stunt to raise awareness for climate change, but Bryan's iffy on it. He'll probably make me do something on a quick turnaround instead."

"Well, at least you have a beat," Christina grumbles. "I'm going to be stuck on the copy desk forever."

I attempt to offer her a reassuring smile. "You'll get there soon enough."

"I know," she reluctantly agrees. "Or at least, I hope."

Christina, once an overeager and talented intern, simply refused to let the editorial team end her time with the company once she graduated college last spring. She petitioned the editors and HR department until she got an offer letter for a full-time job. But since there weren't any reporting openings, she got assigned to the copy desk—and has been somewhat miserable there ever since.

And, unfortunately, part of my daily routine is listening to her whine about it.

She decided early on that we were going to be friends, despite the almost decade age gap between us, but I've been a somewhat reluctant participant.

"I've started pitching stories, actually." Christina bounces slightly with excitement. "Diana on features was telling me—"

"Dakota," Bryan calls, stepping out of his office. "Can you come in here for a minute?"

"Sure," I say as I stand up and smooth down my skirt.

"Uh, oh," Christina exhales as she watches him retreat.

"What?" I balk.

"Calling you in for a meeting before deadline," she

warns like she has some big inside scoop. "Nothing good can come of that."

I wave her off. "Such a pessimist. It'll be fine."

"Can I tell you about my story ideas over lunch? Maybe you could tweak my pitch?"

I was really hoping to get a jumpstart on my next story while scarfing down a granola bar at my desk, but she looks at me with such wide, hopeful eyes that I feel compelled to help her out.

"Okay," I agree.

"Great!" She hops off my desk and practically skips back over to her side of the newsroom.

I take a long, deep breath to focus myself as I walk into Bryan's office.

It's something I've done hundreds of times before, so while I'm rarely caught off guard with his beckoning me in, I'm curious as to what the reason is today. I can't imagine he's annoyed at Christina's chitchat, even though it's within his earshot, so I try to decipher his mood and what else might have caused it before he even speaks.

I've been around long enough to know his tells—like how when he's nervous he taps his fingers on his desk or how he lets his candy bar wrappers and Diet Coke cans stack up when he's stressed out.

Thankfully, there's no fidgeting or garbage to take in when I sit down across from him.

And, even more intriguing, he actually looks...somewhat cheerful, which is definitely not the norm.

"What's up?" I ask cautiously.

Bryan leans back in his chair, lacing his fingers together

to hold his head up as he stares me down. "How's the Ellison piece looking?"

"Good," I answer. "I was just giving it a final pass before the web team formats it."

He nods. "I know you have a laundry list of ideas of what you want to do next, not to mention at least five follow-ups that you could do from this story alone, but I had an assignment drop on my lap that you're going to be taking on."

I blink at his directive masked in a casual tone.

We usually go back and forth on ideas, kicking them around and arguing over approaches before I run with whatever we agree on.

It's unlike him to speak in absolutes, and I can't say I'm a fan of this.

"What's that?" I ask, tone neutral.

"Travis Young."

His two words are simple, but they're heavy with expectation.

And that's when the proverbial ominous clouds roll in.

I grind my molars together. "What about him?"

"You're familiar with him, I assume," Bryan questions, even though he knows the answer.

Because what living, breathing person my age *hasn't* heard of Travis Young?

I nod. "Of course."

"It's been years since he's granted an in-depth interview." He shifts in his seat, resting his elbows on his desk. "In fact, he's known for having a bit of a temper with the press, especially when they try to dig. I believe he even called a *Post* reporter a 'goddamn cockroach,' when asked about a past relationship."

"Watching celebrity interviews isn't exactly how I spend my free time," I say flatly.

Bryan snorts. "No? I'm shocked."

"So I can't exactly say I'm familiar with this."

"Even then, you can probably imagine my surprise when his publicist reached out to me, pitching a feature story on Travis that coincides with the release of his newest album." He hitches his body forward, practically lying on top of his desk to drive his point home. "And that she asked for you, by name, to write the story."

"That's surprising," I allow, a little dumbfounded.

"And you know what I said to her very absurd request?"

I level my gaze on him. "What?"

"Of course we're going to fucking do it!" Bryan laughs at his own crassness. "We'd be insane to turn it down. Even for as little as I care for the pop-punk, or whatever bullshit he's hawking, the exposure for our little media brand would be incredible."

"Well, I hope one of Diana's feature reporters enjoys writing about him," I say lightly as I stand up, making a show of my disinterest. "If you'll excuse me, I have actual *reporting* to do."

"Sit down," Bryan snaps.

I cross my arms over my chest and refuse to oblige out of principle.

But I don't walk away.

"Come on, don't be a snob, Dakota," he scoffs. "Now that you're about to publish the Ellison story, you think general assignments are beneath you? There was once a time you would have taken any story I gave you with a smile on your face."

I glare at him. "I respect you enough not to point out how insulting that is."

"Fine," he breathes. "But that doesn't change anything. You're going to take the story. Frankly, you'd be stupid not to. It's going to be killer for your career."

"Oh, great, a career-killer?" I fire back.

He rolls his eyes. "You know what I mean."

"How the hell is doing a piece on some drunken musician going to do anything for anyone other than help a record label make more money? If I wanted to do something that soulless, I would have taken a corporate job."

"It's a fucking *feature story*, Dakota, not the end of the world."

I pinch the bridge of my nose as I try to compose myself. "It's a conflict of interest."

"Out of all the ridiculous excuses I've heard from reporters over the years, I never expected you'd—"

"We went to high school together," I cut in.

That shuts him up, so I continue without interruption.

"If I recall correctly, his house was about a ten-minute drive from mine, and in eleventh grade, a teacher caught him getting a hand job in the science lab."

Bryan actually laughs at that. "Well, at least his brand has long been consistent with a rockstar persona."

"I don't know why you're being so flippant about this," I say, somewhat dejected.

"Because this story will be big for us, and for whatever reason, they only want you to tell it."

"That doesn't even make sense," I argue. "I don't think

we've ever actually spoken, but now he gets to demand my time and attention? To get some coverage of some album release that's going to smash the charts with or without my efforts?"

Bryan chuckles at my irritation. "So, by your own admission, it's *not* a conflict of interest. You don't even know him."

If I had a pillow, I would scream into it right now.

"Look, Dakota," Bryan softens his tone. "I know this isn't normally your thing, but this could be good for you. Just like when I had to travel to Tahiti—"

"Not the Tahiti story," I groan. "I don't want to relive your reporting glory days or hear about the time you got chlamydia. Again."

"The point I'm trying to make here is that you're going to do it," he presses on. "It's going to challenge you, I know, but it could be—"

"Don't you dare say 'fun,' Bryan," I snap.

He puts his hands up in a defensive position. "Wouldn't dream of it."

I dig my fingertips into my hips as I process all this information.

While I've seen the adult Travis Young enough times on billboards and the occasional YouTube video, I can't think of anything in our very limited shared history that would cause these events to unfold.

In fact, if he hadn't gone on to become famous, I doubt I would even remember his name.

We maybe had a handful of classes together over the years, and while his priorities mostly consisted of feeling up one of his many girlfriends or sneaking cigarettes in between classes, I was a diligent student, already the wannabe, obsessive reporter that I consider myself to be now.

Why would Travis Young ask for me, of all people, to do a story on him?

It seems somehow too familiar yet too random, but maybe I'm overthinking it.

Perhaps his publicist saw my writing, liked my style, and thought I'd be a good fit to tell whatever story they're trying to push.

Those things considered, I'm slightly intrigued about this entire endeavor.

As if my own mind wants to justify accepting the assignment, I recall my favorite professor once emphasizing the importance of not letting our writing or our subjects get stale. In that vein, it might be nice to get a break from my normal beat and cover someone with a much shorter rap sheet and fewer human rights violations.

I clear my throat. "So, the direction is focused on his upcoming album?"

He fist-pumps, not at all slyly, under his desk. "Yes."

"I haven't agreed yet," I remind him firmly. "But are there any terms and conditions?"

"I'm glad you asked," he says with glee.

He slides his chair back and grabs a sizable stack of papers from the printer.

"His legal team sent over about a dozen non-disclosure forms," Bryan explains. "And before you say anything, yes, I know it's not standard practice, but the NDA doesn't inhibit the story. The label wants you to have first listen of his new album, hence all the secrecy."

"They think we'd leak it?" I guess.

He shrugs. "Who knows what they think, but you'll need to sign all those documents. Legal already reviewed them."

With a sigh, I grab a pen off his desk and start marking the pages with my swirling signature. "What else are they expecting from this story?"

"What do you mean?"

"Surely they think it will drum up some press, good or bad, but I'm curious as to what they're hoping for," I say. "Exposure? Change of image? A fluff piece? Making friends with the media?"

"I have no idea, but surely my best reporter can let me know when she figures it out."

I press my lips into a flat line to keep from smiling. "Will do, boss."

TWO

One of the few perks of taking this story is that I'm able to ditch Christina's lunch invitation under the guise of doing research.

But after a day of not feeling like myself, along with the complete but temporary pivot in my career, I let her talk me into going out for drinks after work.

It's not something I indulge in regularly, and I'm reminded of that clearly enough by her instant shock at my agreement. I also don't think she takes her eyes off me until we're sitting side by side at a bar not too far from our office.

Even then, she regards me tentatively, like I'm going to flee at any moment.

"This is a cause for a celebration," Christina declares when we've settled in.

"The Ellison piece or my going out?" I ask.

She chuckles. "Both. Let's do a shot!"

I groan internally but don't decline as she engages with the bartender.

My partying days have long passed, and I don't think I've stayed out past midnight since college—something that Christina thinks is a sin given that bars are open until four in the morning here in the city.

"What is this?" I ask as the bartender slides six shots in front of us. "And how drunk are we planning on getting?"

She grins. "Tequila. And plenty. And here's to you kicking ass at work."

"And to you getting your first story one day," I add.

"Hopefully it involves tagging along with hot rockstars," she says enviously. "You're honestly living my dream."

I smile tightly as we clink glasses. "Bottoms up."

"Oh," she coughs after we take back our shots. "Awful."

My eyes water as I suck on a lime wedge, trying to cut the burn and taste of alcohol.

"Maybe we should have started with mixed drinks," Christina laments, even though she immediately reaches for her second one.

I exhale long and deep, but the sound is dampened by the techno music playing a fraction too loudly through the speakers.

"So, are you nervous at all?" Christina asks me. "Excited? God, I can't even imagine what it's going to be like."

I shrug. "I'm neutral about it. Equal parts intrigued over what to expect and annoyed that I have to push back my other assignments."

She snickers. "I'm sure there will be plenty of hard-hitting stories waiting after you follow around Travis freakin' Young for a week."

"But I'm going to miss out catching the onslaught of coverage and pressing interest after my piece launches. It's time for me to double down on follow-ups, not scale back." I stop and frown. "Who knows what will happen, though. It's not like I have any information that the FBI doesn't. I mean, they have the power to dig into back accounts and subpoena people—"

"Stop," Christina implores. "Please, Dakota, we're at a bar, and you're talking about subpoenas."

"It's not like I've had a personality transplant since we crossed the threshold," I grumble. "You know what you signed up for."

"Then you're going to need this," she says, nudging the second shot toward me. "Because you should know what *you* signed up for."

"What's that?" I ask tentatively before I down it.

She smiles over my shoulder, and I turn to see several people I recognize from the sales team.

"Christina," I say with a slight whine. "You didn't."

"What? Ryan asked what I was doing tonight, and I didn't want to lie."

"So you extended an invitation?"

"Why waste a night out with just the two of us?" she says flippantly before standing to greet one of the guys. "It's not like you've been with anyone since Mark, anyway. Lighten up."

I have pretty thick skin, cultivated over years of being on the receiving end of red-line edits and unwanted comments on social media, but her slight is delivered so genuinely, it takes me a minute to process.

Once I do, it feels like I've been slapped in the face.

Maybe my reaction is a little aggressive and even childish. I just didn't think spending time with a work acquaintance was a "waste" or that she'd weaponize my failed relationship—and subsequent string of hookups with my ex-boyfriend—to get me to indulge.

Then again, I see how Christina shines even brighter under the additional attention and immediately am reminded of why she put me in this position.

She lives for a social setting, smiling and preening when someone offers to buy her a drink, while I sit back and eye my third shot.

The difference in our ages and personalities has never been clearer to me than in this moment, and I'm suddenly glad I didn't open up to her about my confusion over my next project. Something tells me it would have only made this feel worse.

"And, of course, you all know Dakota," Christina says, happy to play hostess for this impromptu work mixer.

I remember being twenty-two and totally carefree, and while sometimes I miss being able to sleep in my makeup without worry of acne or down junk food without fretting over every calorie, I'd never exchange the wisdom I have now for the ignorance of being in that decade again.

It's not like being thirty-one makes me some sort of wise elder in life, but it's old enough to have the confidence to not stick around in a social situation when I could be at home in bed.

I stand up, grab my bag, and smooth my skirt. "Christina," I say, trying to call for her attention, but she's already wrapped up in conversation.

Ryan, who I've met at a few company events, grins my way at the sound of my voice, probably suspecting he's found an opening. He's one of those classically handsome types, with a trendy, tailored, button-down shirt and just the right amount of hair gel that it could pass as being naturally messy.

"Hi," he greets before leaning in for a hug.

I reluctantly accept the embrace and overpowering cologne while wondering if he can smell the lingering effects of my coffee bath this morning.

"Dakota, right?"

"Right," I confirm.

I don't like that he felt comfortable enough going in for a hug when he didn't even know my name for certain.

He nods. "Cool. I should buy you a drink."

I shake my head. "No, thanks. I'm fine."

"I insist," he presses. "You're the reason I had such a good day."

"I am?" I can't help but ask.

"The Ellison story is bringing in a shit ton of traffic," he answers as he waves the bartender over.

I pick up the third and final shot Christina ordered for me, along with another lime wedge, and wonder how bad of an idea it would be to take it.

Probably very terrible.

But I do anyway, and I immediately feel the effects, compounding on the tequila already making its way through my system on an empty stomach.

"That's a very precise unit of measurement, Ryan. Shit ton?"

He chuckles. "Well, we sold out all our ad space for the rest of the month, so I, for one, am in the mood to celebrate."

That's news to me.

But there tends to be a clear line of divide between the editorial and sales departments to maintain our objectivity in reporting, and in this context, ignorance is bliss.

I have enough to deal with, managing my own workload and the mentions and shares of my story on my personal social media accounts, so I don't bother worrying about the company's numbers. I just do my job and try to continue getting information from sources while building my network.

"What can I order for you?" Ryan asks.

"I'm good."

His brow furrows. "No, really. I'm buying."

"I'm fine," I promise, feeling a little looser than I intended to. "Thank you, though."

"Oh, come on," he goads, tapping his credit card on the surface of the bar.

I drop my gaze, finding his encouragement eerily similar to the one I heard this morning right before the coffee guy called me a bitch.

And suddenly, with that reminder, my entire body feels heavy and exhausted from the day's events.

Too many things out of the norm have happened for me to process, and all I want to do is be alone until I have to try again tomorrow.

"I'm actually heading out," I tell him.

Ryan's face falls, but he quickly finds his composure. "That's a shame."

"Uh-huh," I grunt, slinging my purse over my shoulder.

"Well, I'll see you around," he says, already scanning the bar for someone else to charm.

"Yep." I turn. "See you later, Christina."

I say the words loudly enough that I finally get her attention, and she nearly falls off the stool when she reaches for me.

"Don't leave," she says with a pout.

I shake my head as I reach into my wallet.

"Stay, come on. It'll be fun."

After pulling out a few bills, I thrust them toward her. "For the drinks."

"Another round," she yells, not even in the direction of the bartender.

Our coworkers chuckle around her, enthralled by her lively personality, and I leave before she can try to ply me with more alcohol.

She won't even miss me, and I'm totally fine with that. I'm happy in my own company as I step outside into the air that is *just* the right amount of warm.

I feel invigorated as I walk toward the subway station, then I spend the entirety of the ride back to Manhattan thinking about how good it's going to feel to shower and curl up in bed.

But surprisingly, by the time I drag myself all the way home, bathe, and begin stuffing my face with leftover fettuccine, I'm wide awake.

I open my laptop with the intention of mindlessly

scrolling on social media until my brain tires out, but as I open a new tab, my email pings.

And even though it's late and I'm buzzed as hell, I open it to find correspondence directly from the record label with a personal link to listen to Travis Young's new album, *Honest Chaos*.

And I have to hear it.

Right now.

Every single part of me is compelled to listen at this moment, so I curl up on the couch with my laptop propped up on a pillow and hit play.

The first song starts slow, vocals and the slightest strumming on guitar, lulling me through the first few lines until the drums kick and it transforms into something else completely. I'm jolted by the increase in volume, but after my heart stops pounding in surprise, I can appreciate how well it finishes out before the next song starts.

Each track on the album seems to build on the one before it, like he's telling a complete story of his life within these different sets of lyrics and melodies, and by the time I finish my first listen of the ten tracks, I decide I actually really like it.

When I listened to snippets of his earlier records at my desk this afternoon, I mentally labeled his style as guitar-heavy pop-punk with a whining tone to it.

But this is different.

Better, I think.

I'm not a music connoisseur by any means. I have two music apps on my phone solely dedicated to listening to podcasts, and I was a teenager the last time I attended a concert—which is why my knowledge of musical theory and the latest styles is a little limited.

So given my lack of expertise, the best way I can classify Travis Young's sound is that he's somehow mixed the vocalization and catchiness of Blink-182 with the garage-rock instrumental and raw lyrical styling of The Strokes' first album—the first and last physical CD I ever purchased.

I don't know how the hell he is making that delicious, heavy sound on his guitar with these new songs, but damn, even I'm impressed.

I move to my bed for the second listen through, and once I confirm my opinion, I want to know more.

About the evolution of the music.

About how his band makes it all go.

About the three-year refusal to talk to the press.

About him.

Sometimes, being a journalist toes the line of stalking, but I give myself permission to find out everything I can about Travis Young under the guise of research. Although, normally when I do this professionally, I turn to sources other than gossip sites and YouTube, but this is where my tequila-addled brain wants to start.

It's innocent enough at first.

I watch all his music videos, chuckling slightly at some of his early stuff, which was clearly filmed on a shaky camera in our hometown.

Back then, his lyrics focused on wanting to make it big, recounting all the women he slept with and the cash he blew.

Honestly, being a writer, I can't say his lyrical craft has evolved much over time, but the dynamic has shifted into deeper territory, showing a more vulnerable and raw version of himself.

I can understand why he's popular.

Also, I do have two working eyes, which means I can literally *see* why. He's sexy in the grungy sort of way. His limbs are long and lean, but he carries himself with surprising grace as he screams into the microphone on stage.

Plus, he's confident as hell, wearing shirts unbuttoned enough to reveal an obscene number of tattoos.

I'm embarrassingly mesmerized watching him run his ring-clad fingers through his overgrown black hair as his piercing blue eyes stare down the camera.

I can't physically handle watching him perform any longer, so I pull up videos of him enduring interviews and interacting with fans.

There's something alluring about how genuine he seems in talking about his music and the people who support him, but it's clear he hates the people who take videos of him running errands or asking him questions that don't involve his work.

Which absolutely does not bode well for my latest endeavor.

Neither does the spike in my blood pressure as I take in the various women he appears to have on rotation, clinging to his arm at various events, and the many bras that end up on the stage at the end of his performance.

Even worse, among the vast number of videos, I come across a clip of him downing a shot, then spitting it into a girl's mouth, which I find equal parts disgusting and erotic.

I drop my head back against my pillow and rub my eyes.

What the actual *fuck* is wrong with me?

I'm a reporter at a well-known publication—not some fangirl fawning over a rockstar.

But as I fall asleep, all the content I just took in replays in my mind, and my last conscious thought is that I might actually not totally hate this assignment.

THREE

Coffee and a few pills stave off any remnants of a hangover, but I'm still not exactly in the best mood when I show up to the office the next day.

At least Christina's not at her desk, so I don't have to feign interest in her gossip and brush off her attempt at guilt for leaving early last night.

But just as I've gotten comfortable in my own space, Bryan calls me into his office.

I don't even get to appreciate the coverage and chatter about my Ellison article—aside from my deep dive into my social media mentions on the train ride here—because I'm immediately pulled into all things Travis Young.

"Give me an update on your research," he says, eyes focused on whatever's on his laptop screen.

"I've listened to all of his music, watched the majority of his music videos, suffered through a number of interviews and paparazzi shots, and read a fair amount of coverage on him over the years."

"Good. What'd you think of his new album?"

I tilt my head. "It's not my place to have an opinion on it."

"I'm asking as an interested party, not your boss who expects you to maintain your journalistic impartiality at this moment."

"It's..." I trail off, searching for the most appropriate description. "Pretty okay."

Bryan looks directly at me. "Did it physically pain you to say something nice about this assignment?"

"Maybe," I deflect, withholding a smile.

He shakes his head. "Well, I just got the schedule from Leigh, who is our PR contact with Travis Young. I just forwarded it to you, so you have all the times and addresses, but today, you get the privilege of tagging along to a meeting with the record label. Then over the next few days, you'll attend a party for the new unisex shoe line he's the face of, hang around set while he films a music video, and attend a handful of other meetings and events as part of his entourage."

"His *entourage*?" I deadpan, evoking an eyeroll from Bryan. "I've noticed you haven't mentioned any specifically planned interview times. Is that something I'll have to work in myself, or do you just want a recap of the events as they unfold?"

Bryan takes a long sip of coffee. "You've made your stance on this assignment crystal clear, Dakota, but if this were any other topic, something you actually give a shit about, how would you approach it?"

I actually think I've been fairly neutral this morning, which is fairly impressive, given how my thoughts wandered last night, but I swallow any residual attitude and answer his question honestly.

"Out of everything I've processed in the last day, it's clear to me that the public has bought into the persona he has created for himself."

"And from the way you phrased that, I'm guessing you haven't?" Bryan prompts.

I shrug. "He, or whoever is around him, meticulously crafted his wild image early in his career. There are so many videos and pictures of him stumbling out of clubs and bars, but in the last few years, even before he went MIA, most of the coverage includes fuzzy still images and quotes from 'reliable sources.'"

"And now?"

"I don't know if he lost his edge, shunned it completely, or is making a tactical move."

It could be all of the above, really, given that his new album is a pivot from his last few, but I just don't know enough yet.

Bryan watches me process this. "Interesting."

"Well, it's just if I were some rich, sexy, and talented musician who makes a living off of being seen and heard, why would I scorn extra attention?" I speculate, thinking out loud. "You don't exactly become famous by being a homebody."

"So you're going to write a profile, then?"

"I just want the truth," I admit carefully. "I don't want to feed into what gets him album sales, even if that's what the label wants. I want to understand *him*."

"Then do it," Bryan says with an encouraging wave. "That meeting starts at ten o'clock."

I blink, suddenly feeling grossly unprepared. "In an hour?"

"Yep."

I pull up the agenda on my phone. "In *Midtown*?" I shriek. "The trains are going to be a mess!"

Bryan shrugs. "Good luck."

With a sound of frustration, I beeline for my desk, shove my laptop, charger, and all the other essentials into my bag, then I bolt to the subway.

It's not the disruption in my routine that I'm irritated about, because I expected that, but how last minute this is. I hate rushing and the general feeling of being late and on edge, and worse, the platform in the station is completely packed.

I have to let two trains completely filled with people go by before one stops that I can get on.

Thankfully, there are no delays as we cross the East River, and once we're back underground, winding underneath Manhattan, I check the time on my phone every thirty seconds. Once I get off at the correct stop, I get turned around on the streets and end up passing the building entrance.

I make it inside with five minutes to spare, and a security guard in a maroon blazer smiles at me.

"Meetings rarely start on time here," he says encouragingly as he hands my driver's license back to me.

"Thanks," I say, exhaling in relief.

"You're all set on the forty-second floor." He points toward the elevator bank. "Good luck."

"I appreciate it."

I follow his direction, finding the contrast of this

skyscraper to our little three-floor building in Brooklyn almost laughable.

In the few movies I've watched that are supposed to be based in New York, all the characters work at places like this with sleek décor and men clad in expensive suits.

I try to appreciate the sound of my most comfortable pair of heels clacking against the marble flooring, but I'm too awed by the modern art structures and how chicly all the people around me are dressed. Even the elevators are gigantic and covered with enough mirrors that as people file in, I can still take in my reflection.

Thankfully, my appearance is far better than it was yesterday.

Although I didn't expect to be joining in a formal meeting, my olive-green dress screams business casual and suits the situation just fine. My hair is pin-straight and not too frizzy in the humidity, and I'm able to use the reflection to reapply my lipstick before the doors open on the correct floor.

The receptionist there directs me to the correct conference room, and while it's obviously not as big as the lobby, it's impressive.

I take a seat to the side of the massive glass table, intentionally picking a position prime for people-watching rather than joining in the discussion.

The security guard was right—no one else is on time, which surprises me slightly but also gives me more time to mentally prepare.

I pull up my phone and open my favorite note-taking app, pretending to be enthralled in what I'm reading as the first few attendees file in.

They smile and nod at my presence, but ultimately, I'm left alone as they turn their attention to one another and engage in small talk as they wait for Travis to make his appearance.

And when he finally steps into the room, the chatter dies and everyone zeroes in on him, including me.

His cool demeanor and shredded clothing is an incredible contrast to the pristine setting and prim posture of the executives, but he seems unbothered, merely offering a flippant wave before taking a seat at the head of the table.

He's flanked on either side by Leigh and Devin, his older brother and manager.

The meeting begins when one of the men clears his throat, diving right into pleasantries that Travis barely engages in.

Even with his lack of participation, I can't tear my eyes away from him.

I wish I had any sort of excuse to keep staring at him because he's even better looking in person.

He's still got that same rebellious exterior I recall from high school, but he's grown into his height—six-four, according to the internet—and build nicely.

I get a glimpse of his lean muscles every time he shifts in the cushy leather chair, and even the slightest movement of him rolling his head side to side to crack his neck causes a rippling effect.

His eyes wander around the room, landing on each person as they speak, as he uses his thumb to spin the gaudy ring around his forefinger, and I can't help but notice how *large* his hands are.

Holy hell.

I need to get it together.

After letting out a long exhale, I project professionalism in my mind, keeping my expression neutral and artfully intact as I wait, pray, and hope for him to acknowledge my presence.

I blink when I catch the gaze of Leigh, who smiles at me reassuringly as one of the executives stands and starts talking in the most monotone voice I've ever heard.

And doesn't stop.

For forty fucking minutes.

I'm normally a sucker for data and planning, but I can barely focus on the distribution numbers, "chart potential" statistics, and other topics. My fingers fly on my phone, jotting down random snippets of information to keep my mind occupied.

"What do you think, Leigh?" He finally ends his monologue and asks for feedback. "Does this fall in line with what you're planning for promo this week?"

"Absolutely," she enthuses with multiple head nods. "I already have social posts and graphics lined up to push out across his accounts, as well as a number of events he'll attend and be photographed at over the next few days. And you've probably noticed our guest…"

I sit up a fraction straighter as she gestures to me.

"This is Dakota Shaw, the senior reporter at *Exos*. She's going to be with us every step of the way as we get ready to launch, and we're hoping to time the article with the start of the tour. No promises, of course, since it's their call."

"We'll see what we can do," I say lightly.

Leigh grins. "Thank you."

Then she turns back to the table and continues on.

I'm instantly relieved to have the attention off of me, only for it to be the exact moment Travis finally acknowledges my presence, his blue eyes locking onto my hazel ones.

I shiver under the intensity of his gaze, and just as I'm trying to decide if it's a look of annoyance, anger, or curiosity, he shuts me out.

He reaches into his back pocket and pulls out a little black notebook with a pen attached to the cover.

It looks comically small in his hands, but he's unbothered by it, only half-listening to the conversation that resumes around him as he swirls words on the page.

Leigh continues her assessment, spouting viral tactics and referring to a few previous campaigns they've run, and the suits all agree with her that with Travis's being mostly out of the public eye for the last few years, this album will make an even bigger splash.

Only a few reputable publications documented Travis's sudden disappearance, speculating on the cause being label disputes or even rehab. Since then, most of the gossip articles and social media posts pertaining to him have been grainy phone pictures or paparazzi stills of him grocery shopping, eating dinner with various companions, or doing other mundane human tasks.

I'm hoping to be the one who gets to dig a little deeper and unpack what is really going on.

For the next hour, I continue taking notes just for something to do. I already know I won't use much, if any, of the content of this meeting in the article. But it does set the tone of the dynamic between Travis, his publicist, the label, and his brother-slash-manager, who has been swiping on a dating app under the table but in my direct line of sight since the moment he sat down.

Mostly, I'm just dying to know what Travis is scrawling in his notebook.

My fingers itch to flip through those pages, to take in the stream of consciousness, but the way he holds it out of view from everyone and tucks it into his pocket for safe-keeping as the meeting adjourns…I have a feeling it's not something he shares with many people, if anyone at all.

"Hey," Leigh says, stepping in front of me. "Dakota. I'm Leigh Baker. Travis's publicist."

I blink, clearing my vision after a few minutes of staring off into space. "Nice to officially meet you," I tell her, standing up and extending my hand.

She shakes it as a wide smile spreads across her face. "And you, of course. I read your story on that piece of shit Ellison on the cab ride over here. Incredible work as always."

"Thank you," I say automatically.

"I know this week is going to be a little different than what you're accustomed to," she says, stating the obvious. "But Travis and I really wanted you specifically on this story."

"And why is that, exactly?" I ask as she leads me toward the elevator.

"Because you're *you*."

I can feel the skepticism mar my features. "What does that mean?"

"You're the best," she says like it's the most obvious thing in the world.

I don't think that's true.

I'm not being modest about it—I know there are more seasoned reporters in both feature writing and investigative reporting that would probably be thrilled to have the opportunity to talk to Travis and follow him along on his errands.

But even if I don't believe her explanation, it would be ridiculous for me to argue with her, so I drop it.

"Oh, sorry," she says to me as she pulls her trilling phone out, then answers it quickly. "Yes. Yep. We're on the way down. We'll be there in like thirty seconds. I know. We'll have plenty of time. Okay. Bye."

The elevator doors open to a spacious underground garage—something I hadn't guessed would be underneath the massive building—and I can't help but whistle at the number of expensive cars housed here.

"You're okay to come along with us, right?" Leigh asks.

"Sure. But to where, exactly?"

"Two stores in lower Manhattan are holding pieces for Travis," she explains. "One of his bags got lost on the way here, and of course it's the one he needs for a shoot. I guess that's what we get for flying commercial."

"Right," I say, feigning like I can relate to anything at all she just said.

"This is us," Leigh says brightly.

She gestures toward an oversized black van with tinted windows, which I associate with the one bachelorette party I was coerced into attending during my early days at *Exos*.

I slide into the expansive leather seat next to hers, expecting some sort of introduction to Devin and Travis, but once the driver shuts the door, we're off in relative silence.

Leigh takes another phone call, arguing with the person at the other end because, apparently, it's a big debate on whether to exclude dill from whatever hors d'oeuvres are being served at Travis's shoe launch party.

Directly behind me, Devin listens to music on his wireless headphones loud enough that I can pick up the sound of the bass.

And the gaze of the man in question is fixed out the window, watching the people, buildings, and bustle of Manhattan fly by.

Rarely am I in a position that I don't know what to do with myself, especially while in the middle of chasing a story, so I feel a little out of my element.

In hopes of getting my bearings, and not looking completely lost, I pull my phone out of my purse and check the schedule. Tonight is blocked off for "personal time," but I note that the next few days are pretty busy.

Without even knowing what people wear to launch parties, I'm already certain that nothing in my closet will help me fit in with that crowd. Travis's jeans have more holes in them than actual stitching, whereas I've carefully curated a capsule wardrobe, which is why losing my favorite white button-down to the coffee bath was like a punch in the gut.

I also have a hunch that the store we're speeding toward won't be in the realm of my price range, not to mention it'd be really inappropriate for me to try on clothing while in the process of interviewing someone.

Speaking of which…

I turn back around and glance at Travis expectantly.

He chews on his bottom lip, but he doesn't look over, even after I clear my throat.

"Travis," I say clearly and full of confidence.

That, at least, earns me the privilege of eye contact.

"What's up?"

"Can we talk?" I ask, wishing my question didn't sound so pathetic.

The eyebrow with the metal bar through it ticks upward, like he's mildly amused that I'm asking for his attention. "About what?"

"You."

He hitches his shoulders in a quick shrug. "Pass."

"Excuse me?" I sputter in disbelief.

"Maybe later," he says dismissively. "Now's not a good time."

"Travis," I grit out slowly. "I'm here to interview *you* for the release of *your* new album."

His only response is to sit back in his seat and close his eyes.

My instinct is to fire back at him, but I kill that impulse, even though the irritation makes my heart pound.

I have days to corner him and get him to open up, I remind myself, and this isn't my normal, somewhat straightforward beat. I'm not setting up interviews with the intention of drilling sources with questions—I have to take my time here, warm up the subject before I try and pull all sorts of personal details out of him.

At least, that's what I mentally say to make myself feel better.

After twenty minutes of stop-and-go traffic, we park in front of a trendy-looking boutique.

The driver slides open the door for us, and I barely take in the exceptionally well-dressed mannequins in the window before flashbulbs begin going off in my face.

"Travis! Travis! Over here."

Five photographers appear out of nowhere in an attempt to document Travis's walk from the van to the front door.

"What the hell?" I say, blinking as white spots float in my vision.

Leigh locks her arm through mine. "The boutique must have tipped them off," she huffs, pulling me inside. "Fucking publicity hounds."

I guffaw at that statement, finding it odd from someone whose entire job is publicity, but Leigh doesn't notice, simply waving off the paparazzi and closing the door as quickly as she can.

One of the store employees pushes a button that lowers privacy shades over the windows, effectively neutralizing the paparazzi before turning to greet Travis.

"Mr. Young," she says brightly. "I was thrilled when we got the call that you were interested in some of our pieces. And you must be Leigh."

Leigh smiles at her, but it's not exactly genuine. "We appreciate you accommodating us on such short notice."

"I'm Devin, Travis's manager and more handsome older brother," Devin says with a wink that makes me cringe internally.

The employee beams at him. "Well, I've set some pieces aside in the dressing room for Travis, but feel free to browse and let me know if there's anything you need."

I'm glad to be spared an introduction, since it gives me a chance to direct my clearing vision around the store.

I take in the mix of modern and vintage patterned pieces and file the shop in the category of places I've always admired but rarely stepped foot in. I wander around, mentally cataloging the vibe and how this style fits in with Travis's persona as I drag my fingertips across the various fabrics.

This type of store is where people who have a distinct style shop to build a wardrobe with different looks that scream to be photographed.

There's a delicate slip dress on display at the front of the store, and I can't help but picture what I would look like in it. The cut is beautiful, but the lemon yellow would clash awfully with my fair hair, and wearing such thin fabric in public would make me incredibly self-conscious.

But we're not here for me, which is even more obvious when I catch the number of zeroes on the price tag for a tiny crop top.

I have to actively withhold the laughter threatening to spill out of my mouth.

"This is ridiculous," I mutter, and I'm not just talking about the prices.

I shift my focus over to Travis, the entire reason I'm here instead of doing my *actual* job.

He messes up a neat pile of logo shirts before moving on to examine a rack of leather jackets, hovering for a minute on one with patches on the back.

"You like that one the best?" I ask him, trying to break the ice.

"If I say yes, are you going to include that in the write-up?" Travis says flippantly.

He manages to say the words without a shred of emotion, good or bad, which is just as impressive as it is frustrating.

"Maybe." I try to channel his nonchalance, but it comes off sharply.

"Then 'maybe' is my answer, too," he retorts with the ghost of a smirk on his face.

He abruptly turns and crosses to the other side of the store.

"You said the dressing room's in the back?" Travis asks, interrupting the conversation between Devin, Leigh, and the employee.

"Y-yes," she says. "Can I help you with something?"

He grins at her before he heads that way, which grates at my nerves because it's daggers for me and smiles for complete strangers, apparently.

But then again, I've been around enough classist, rich people who brush off us *normal* workers, so I actually kind of appreciate his friendliness toward her.

I just don't get his angle or whatever game he's playing, and that's truly what's frustrating about this situation.

He specifically asked for *me* to do this story only to string me along?

I don't put up with this type of cat-and-mouse game in relationships, so I'm certainly not going to stand for it in my career—the thing that I've worked harder for than anything else in my life.

At that thought, my dwindling thread of patience snaps.

"Fuck this," I mutter as I stomp down the hallway to the back of the store.

I pull back the heavy velvet curtain of the fitting room just as Travis slips off his shirt.

He seems unfazed by my sudden appearance, and I can't decide if it's because he doesn't give a shit about modesty or because he expected me to follow him.

I force my gaze to stay on his face rather than wandering down his body or studying his tattoos. "Why am I here, Travis?"

He grabs a printed silk shirt and slides it on. "You tell me."

"Cut the bullshit," I demand. "I have a job to do. You asked for me specifically, and now you're brushing me off? It doesn't make sense."

He eyes himself in the mirror. "Not my problem."

I step over, blocking his view. "Is this a part of your brand? Acting all nonchalant to reporters so they say you're some sort of untouchable being? Because that's not going to work on me."

Wordlessly, he unbuckles his belt. "Again, not my problem."

I grit my teeth in irritation. "Do you even remember me, Travis?"

"Barely." He offers me a challenging look as he kicks off his jeans. "Just a general recollection of you being a pain in the ass know-it-all."

"Well, you were the stoner who barely attended enough classes to graduate," I snap.

This is so unbelievably unprofessional on both of our accounts, but I don't intend on backing down.

"And yet we both turned out just fine," he says evenly. "Well, mostly."

I balk at those words, unsure of what he's implying. "Mostly?"

Travis quirks an eyebrow as if the answer is obvious.

"Are you implying that money and fame is the end goal for everyone?" I scoff. "That people don't have other desires or better things to do than get high and go scream on a stage while people grope one another?"

I stop before I get ahead of myself and take a breath, lowering the volume of my voice.

"I'm a *journalist*, Travis. Not some sort of lost puppy following you around New York."

He runs his hands through his overgrown hair. "Good to know."

My betraying eyes drop down to the fabric of his boxer briefs and the exposed skin of his abdomen.

I inhale before I drag my eyes upward again. "We barely knew each other in school. This isn't even close to the realm of my expertise, in my beat, or even what I'm interested in. So if you're only going to answer one question today, let it be this one. Why did you want *me* to do this interview?"

Travis steps into a pair of bright red pants and pulls them up.

I can see even in my peripherals that they look absolutely divine, hugging his ass, so I dig my fingertips into my palms to ground myself.

"The label has been pressuring me for interviews for *years*," he says sharply. "I only agreed to do press again if they let me do what I wanted for the album."

"So that makes me, what, some sort of compromise?"

He turns to face me full-on, his blue eyes slicing into me. "Leigh has been babbling on about *Exos* for as long as I've known her, and she thought it was funny that two people from some piece-of-shit town in Pennsylvania went on to live such drastically different lives. I specifically requested you because I never thought you'd agree to it, and we'd both be spared from this absurdity."

"Well, I guess you were wrong," I retort, my voice losing some of its power.

He lets his gaze drop to the ground, and before any other words are exchanged, I turn on my heel and get the hell out of the confined space.

"Now what?" Travis calls after me. "You done?"

"No," I snap. "I'm not quitting. I'm getting to *work*."

He looks mildly taken aback, but there's a note of approval in the way the tension leaves his body.

I'm not entirely surprised at the gawking from the store employees as I head toward the exit, but I do make a point to stop and turn to Leigh.

"I'll see you tomorrow," I promise.

She nods, amusement clear on her features. "I'm looking forward to it."

FOUR

I've spent way too much time in transit today, but the subway ride back to the office helps cool me down.

Not literally, though, because the oppressive late summer heat is awful.

But my mood improves slightly with the help of a massive iced coffee and the donut I shove in my mouth as I walk into the newsroom.

Almost every desk is empty, and I surmise that my colleagues are most likely taking advantage of the sunny afternoon with an early happy hour, enjoying the final wave of summer weather before we're firmly into cooler temperatures.

But, of course, Bryan is in his office.

He offers me a confused look as I huff and drop my bag at my desk.

"I don't want to hear it," I tell him before he can lecture me. "I've had a really shitty day, so I'm going to go back to doing my job until I have to show up to some wasteful, over-the-top party tomorrow."

"Things are going well, then?"

I roll my eyes as I sink into my chair. "I can't believe I'm doing this. Twenty-two-year-old me would have a fit if she saw what a sellout I've become."

"Dakota," Bryan says slowly. "It's *one* assignment."

"One assignment with terrible timing," I argue.

He frowns. "Have you checked social media at all today?"

I perk up at that. "No. Why? Something good? Have more people come forward? Any response from Ellison Incorporated?"

"Not exactly," he says with a grimace.

It's then I notice the six empty Diet Coke cans on his desk.

"It didn't really make the splash that you hoped," he continues. "Not externally, anyway. Some business journals picked it up, and you got a small call-out in the *Times*. But it makes me concerned—"

"That there's more to the story that others have uncovered and are sitting on," I finish for him, then sigh. "Shit."

"I hoped that this was going to be it for you, Dakota. The story that broke and changed your career. But it looks like you have to keep searching for that scoop."

I tug at the ends of my hair. "Good thing I'm wasting my time with Travis Young."

"I wouldn't say that," Bryan pushes back. "Think of this as a palate cleanser to change your perspective, so you can come back to your beat with fresh eyes. You're a hell of a reporter already, but you still have lots to learn."

"Don't patronize me," I say, annoyed.

"And you could stand to let yourself enjoy this entire experience, which I know is a rarity for you." He levels with me. "Don't give me that look. You don't always have to hit readers with cold, hard facts. You can take some creative liberties. Mold yourself to this story and live like a damn rockstar. You'll be back working to save society soon enough."

I blink rapidly, taking in his words.

It's the same line of thinking I've been wandering along, but hearing Bryan say it all but confirms it in my mind.

I'm not going to turn into a fluffy feature writer overnight, but perhaps there's a middle ground I can uncover.

"Maybe you're right," I relent.

He chuckles. "Of course I'm right."

"I'm going about this the wrong way," I say slowly, wringing my hands together. "Travis Young isn't exactly going to spill his secrets to me unprompted over a beer or two. I have to take this slowly. But maybe I can find something without his help."

"Oh?" Bryan questions, but I'm already standing up as my mind moves.

I head back to my desk and pop in my earbuds.

Honest Chaos is what I choose as the soundtrack to my work of digging further into his past.

I've noticed that in many articles over the years, Travis always touts that he's from Pittsburgh. He's occasionally photographed wearing a Pirates hat, and I'm pretty sure he has "412," the city's area code, tattooed on his ribs.

But his claim is not exactly factually accurate.

49

We're from a small suburb north of the city, which means any public record searches from the county where the city is centered might not bring up all the results on Travis.

So, in the well-practiced art of digging into criminal histories, I pull the database for our actual county.

And gasp aloud at what I find.

In between a few speeding tickets and one parking ticket are words I didn't expect to see...

"Legal separation," I murmur before clicking deeper into the public docket.

The records go back to the year we graduated, and I'm a little dumbfounded that he apparently got married right out of high school. I don't recognize the woman's name, but when I cull searches on his then-wife, she has a number of domestic violence charges and one eviction notice.

I go back to Travis's record and start plotting out a chart of court dates and docket entries compared to a timeline of his success. Although they filed for divorce before his first album dropped, it wasn't officially finalized until six years ago, which seems odd.

This is why I tend to only *start* with the facts and available records online.

While I feel I can trust this data, I need backstory filled in by actual people, which is why I need Travis to open up.

Even so, I continue digging through the other nearby counties until, eventually, my eyes widen because another piece of information drops right on my lap.

I've found the reason Travis went into hiding the past three years.

"Holy shit," I breathe, sinking back into my chair.

Travis Young isn't just a rockstar who traveled the globe, sold out stadiums, and smashed numerous chart records...he's on the brink of real jail time.

The number of charges against him is staggering: driving under the influence, possession, resisting arrest, assault of a police officer, obstruction of justice, bribery.

There are pages of logs in the system, records of different hearings, and resolutions for some of the minor charges, including community service and house arrest. But from what I can tell, his next probationary hearing is timed nicely with the day after his scheduled concert in Pittsburgh.

A story on Travis's sordid past would definitely get attention and clicks and probably make Bryan very happy, but I already know it's not the article I'm going to write.

While some other reporter might see this as their big opportunity and run with it, to me, this merely adds another layer of complexity to who Travis Young *really* is.

It's not lost on me that living in the public eye brings immense pressure, and from what I remember about Travis in high school, I doubt he was the most emotionally and mentally prepared to handle it, so it's no surprise he turned to alcohol and drugs to cope and continue the high of performing.

I'm speculating here, of course, but like him, I still have a job to do.

I chew on my lip as I pull out my phone and scroll through my list of contacts, sighing as I hit the correct name.

My finger hovers over the name as dread hits me, but I push it off as I steel myself for the conversation.

"Dakota?" His voice is a little rough, and there's a note of surprise when he says my name.

I run a hand through my hair. "Mark."

There's a beat of silence.

"How are you?" I ask coolly.

He chuckles. "Don't start the conversation by using your 'I want something' voice. It makes me feel used, Dakota."

"I just asked how you're doing," I defend as the reluctant smile spreads on my face. "It's called being polite."

"You're lucky you caught me on a stakeout," he grumbles. "I'm bored as hell. Otherwise, I'd just hang up on you."

He took me along on his job once, and honestly, he's right. It's mind-numbing to sit there for hours on end, totally alert and believing the worst.

"Trying to catch a husband cheating on his wife?" I guess.

"Actually, the opposite. Husband is suspicious because his wife has a *very* sudden interest in taking tennis lessons. Coincides nicely with the hiring of the new twenty-something instructor at their country club."

I snort. "Rich people problems."

"Which reminds me," Mark says. "I saw your article this morning."

"You and I both make a living off of the mistakes of the wealthy."

"We're quite a pair."

I can picture the hopeful look in his eyes and his easy

demeanor as he sits relaxed in the front seat of his pickup truck, and it makes me chew on my bottom lip in irritation.

"Yes," I breathe.

"Stop it. I don't mean anything by it, just that you're still the best ex-girlfriend I've ever had."

"Well, the bar *is* pretty low, Mark."

After all the years we've spent together and apart, I still find the banter with him easy and comfortable, and sometimes, I wish the rest of our relationship was that way, too.

But it's not.

Long distance—him living not too far from my parents' house—proved to be too difficult to stay together but too easy to fall back into hold habits when I visited.

"Anyway," he continues. "Now that you've started the eventual takedown of Ellison Incorporated, what's next?"

"Well," I renew my gaze on my computer screen. "That's actually why I'm calling."

"Why am I not surprised?" Mark says, tone light.

I roll my eyes. "As much as I enjoy catching up with you, I actually do need your help."

"And just how much are you going to pay me to do this free work for you?" Mark teases.

"Did you not just say that I'm the best ex-girlfriend you've ever had? Surely that counts for something."

"Well, the last time you had me do you a favor for a story, I got reprimanded for letting my focus wander out-of-state," he reminds me. "So I'm hoping you've got something that won't earn me a slap on the wrist this time. What do you have for me, Dakota?"

I pause for a moment. "Travis Young."

"The 'Imposter Syndrome' guy?"

"That's the one," I confirm, knowing most people recognize him from his most commercially successful single.

"You're going from taking down a corporate overlord to writing about the guy who wears more eyeliner than you do?"

"Oh, come on, Mark," I chide. "Don't be an agent of the patriarchy. It's perfectly acceptable for men to wear whatever makeup they want. You're just jealous because you couldn't pull it off if you tried."

"Right, if I'm going to mock him for something, it's going to be how he begged the officer ticketing him for public urination to let it slide, promising to serve him unlimited burritos at his day job. Had that big of an attitude *before* he hit it big, so I can't even begin to imagine what he's like now."

"Sounds about right." I groan. "And I somehow got conned into writing a feature for his upcoming album release. I was just doing some vetting, found something *interesting*."

I already know without being able to read Mark's body language that I've piqued his interest.

"Interesting or suspicious?" he clarifies.

"An ex-wife with a drawn-out legal ordeal," I say, dangling the juicy tidbit for him. "You know I'm limited to what I can see on the docket, though."

"And you want your pal Mark to help you out, make some phone calls, do some light private detective work, and see if there's more to it?"

"Well, it wouldn't hurt."

He laughs. "You know, I *should* hang up on you. Didn't

you ghost me after Easter this year? And now you call me for a favor?"

"And your favorite ex-girlfriend thanks you very much," I say quickly, pulling the phone away from my ear to end the conversation. "I'll text you the details. I appreciate you. Bye!"

"You owe me, Dakota," he says just as I hang up the phone.

I smile as I once again press play on *Honest Chaos*, appreciating the irony as I allow myself to get even deeper into the world of Travis Young.

FIVE

I don't know if she's trying to smooth over yesterday's events, but Leigh stays glued to my side as the launch party for the unisex shoe line starts.

And while I appreciate the escort and the number of introductions she's making for me, it's throwing off my entire process of standing on the sidelines and observing as much as I can.

After what feels like fifty handshakes, we make it through the crowd and come to a stop at a table in the back. It's one of those circular booths you see in the movies but never in reality, with bright red leather and a table full of expensive liquor with labels that are too high-end to be familiar to me.

I shift on my uncomfortable heels and wish the music wasn't so damn loud.

"Champagne?" Leigh offers as she pours herself a glass.

"No, thank you," I say, gripping my phone in my hand. "I'm going to jot down some notes before I forget."

"Okay," she says brightly just before being pulled away.

By Leigh's account, I'm sure this event is already a success.

The venue is absolutely packed, and there are so many recognizable celebrities and public figures here, it makes my head spin.

Everyone seems to be having a good time, drinking, chatting, and taking photos—even though it's a little weird that there are shoes everywhere. Matte black sneakers are on pedestals staged throughout the space and projected in a pattern on the walls.

There's even a cake in the footwear's likeness, waiting to get sliced open.

I don't know who the target audience is for these sneakers that cost three hundred dollars, but even though they seem expensive to me, I'm sure I'm the only one in attendance who thinks so.

After all, Travis's friends and tour bandmates are dripping in diamonds and clothing covered in designer logos, so I don't think anyone associated with them is hurting for cash.

As if he can read my thoughts, Nick, the bassist, sits down at the booth beside me.

I don't let his boyish smile or backward hat fool me into thinking he's just a regular person like me, though, because as he reaches for the open champagne, I catch sight of his Cartier watch.

Obviously, such an accessory is laughably far out of my price range, and it makes me even more aware of how buttoned-up and professional I must look, a stark contrast to this setting.

Then again, it might be good to be set apart from the actual attendees because I'm not here to party.

"How's it going?" Nick asks before he takes a swig directly from the bottle of bubbly.

I'm so fixated on his appearance that, at first, I don't catch the—frankly—depressed look on his face.

But when I do see it, I'm a little confused.

"It's okay," I hedge. "How about you?"

He smiles tightly and turns back to the crowd, still clutching the bottle in his fingertips.

It's an awkward gesture, heightened when he shifts uncomfortably, and that's when it hits me.

He's hiding.

From someone or something, I don't know.

I'm aware that we as a society tend to idolize celebrities, thinking they're untouchable. But if I know anything about Travis, and now this person sharing the booth with me tucked in the back, it's that they can be just as fucked up and shy and human as the rest of us.

"I'm having a blast," he mutters sarcastically, rubbing the back of his neck with one hand.

"You look like it."

That makes him laugh. "I'm sure."

"What's wrong?" I can't help but ask.

He takes another long swig, and just looking at him do it gives me a phantom headache.

"Is this on the record?" Nick asks curiously.

I put my elbows on the table and lean toward him. "Does it have to do with *Honest Chaos*, overpriced sneakers, or Travis?"

His eyes soften a fraction. "Not really. But kind of, I guess."

"There you are," Leigh interrupts, sliding up beside Nick. "Antisocial this evening?"

"No," he deflects. "Dakota and I were just having a chat."

Leigh's gaze flickers between us. "About what?"

"I was asking him a little about his history with Travis," I lie quickly. "I was curious as to why Travis used to tour with a full band but now it's just Nick and Phoenix along for the ride."

Nick nods gratefully at me. "And I was about to answer that we've really stripped down for this time around. It gets too exhausting to have to look after that many people. Logistically, this will be easier. Especially with how many cities we're running through in such a short time."

"Thank you," I say politely. "That makes sense."

Leigh holds her glass out for Nick to refill. "You only have to stay for another hour to keep up appearances, then I'll get you a car back to the hotel."

"Thank the fucking lord," he breathes, then shakes his head as he fixes his gaze forward. "I'm so fucking pathetic."

"Maybe don't put that in the article," Leigh says to me with a smile.

I see the instantaneous shift in Nick's demeanor as Travis and Phoenix approach the table.

"Hey, man," Nick says brightly. "Congratulations! They look great. Leigh says my pair is all packed up for me already. Can't wait to wear them."

"Thanks," Travis says curtly. "Hand me the Don Julio, will you?"

Leigh obliges him, sliding it over, then Travis shoots it back directly from the bottle.

"Is there a glassware shortage in this place?" she asks, exasperated.

"Such a stickler, Leigh," Phoenix says.

"They're called manners," Leigh chides him as he waves a server over.

"Can we get some shot glasses, please?" he asks her, oozing charm.

"Of course," she says excitedly.

I don't miss how Phoenix's eyes stay glued to her form as she reaches behind the bar.

"What's your name, love?" Phoenix asks when she returns.

"Ashley," she says, bright red lips fixed into a grin.

"I'm Phoenix, and I'd love it if you joined us."

She glances around, like someone's watching her every move. "I don't want to get in trouble."

"Oh, you won't," Phoenix promises, gently tugging her down next to him.

The giggles she lets out are shrill enough to make Leigh cringe.

"How's the story coming, Dakota?" Travis asks as he pours a shot for himself.

It's the first time he has willingly addressed me and expressed interest in any sort of conversation, and I pretend it doesn't startle me.

"I'm getting some good context and background information, but it'd be even better if you'd answer some questions for me," I tell him honestly.

"I would pay to see that," Phoenix interjects. "You

know how many reporters have reached out to him, begging for an exclusive?"

Leigh nods in agreement. "He's right."

"Don't you feel extra special now?" Travis drawls with a smirk.

I'm not sure how to feel, exactly, about Travis Young teasing me after our little meltdown yesterday.

But maybe this is his way of offering me an olive branch.

"I *love* this song," Ashley squeals as the DJ changes the track.

It's a hard rock tune I don't recognize, but given how most of the attendees start to sing along, it must be popular.

Phoenix chuckles and looks over at Nick, who refuses to meet his gaze.

"This is our band," Phoenix tells Ashley. "Nick and I put out an LP last year before we all got together to record *Honest Chaos*."

"No way," she says, eyes wide.

Travis takes another sip. "Way."

"A one-hit crash and burn," Nick admits to me before giving Phoenix a longing look.

He, of course, misses it because his attention is focused on the woman on his lap, and he's whispering who knows what into her ear.

"Oh," I breathe.

Nick frowns, nods, then chugs a sizable amount of liquid from the bottle.

I don't need exceptional journalistic skills to know there's a story here.

Although I'm personally curious to find out what it is, I'd have to make leaps and bounds to make it in any way applicable to Travis's story. Not only would that be a gigantic waste of time but it feels gross and truly is in no way my business.

I don't think Phoenix—who legally changed his name from Gerard Smith to the one-word moniker years ago—is going to offer any insight, but Nick just might be my *in* to getting an unabridged backstory of the inner workings of this crew, which will be a tremendous help.

"You sure I can't get you anything to drink?" Leigh offers me.

I shake my head. "No thanks."

"Buzzkill," Travis accuses.

"I'm working," I remind him.

He deliberately downs a shot. "So am I."

I open my mouth to argue that our situations are different, but Bryan's words come to the forefront of my mind.

This isn't a traditional assignment, and even if it were, there's something to be said for immersing yourself in the experiment. One of my coworkers just spent a month at a naked commune in Arizona, and although I don't see myself going to those types of extremes for this piece, I know I could stand to relax a little bit.

I grab the bottle of Don Julio from his hands—oh, why does it *always* have to be tequila—and take in Travis's questioning, pierced brow.

I pour it directly down the hatch, and it takes all my self-control to hold a closed-mouth smile instead of succumbing to a wince.

But I think it earns me something.

Not approval, necessarily, but maybe a little bit of leeway and a slight lowering of the massive, solid wall he puts up between himself and other people.

"What are you fuckers doing over here?" Devin shouts, approaching the table with his arms open wide. "Ignoring the fun while the rest of us party on without you?"

"Fair point," Phoenix says before he murmurs something to Ashley.

His words, whatever they are, cause her to beam.

They stumble out of the booth, through the crowd, and onto the small but busy dancefloor, with Devin trailing behind them, pumping his hands up in the air.

"Travis, you should probably catch up with that one executive from—"

"Leigh," he cuts in. "I just need a few minutes where I'm not being asked one thousand questions and forced to make small talk."

She rolls her eyes. "Fine. I'll go do some of that for you."

"You're the best, Leigh." Travis tilts his shot glass toward her in gratitude before he downs it.

She rises from the booth and steps out to make her rounds, and then it's just the three of us.

Me with my phone of notes.

Travis with his ridiculously high alcohol tolerance.

And Nick with his permeating sadness.

Despite what I *should* be focusing on, it's that last one that catches me the most.

"Come on," I say to Nick, and before I can overthink it, I offer him my hand.

"Don't worry about it," he says somewhat dejectedly. "I don't want to ruin your night."

"I'm getting paid to be here, which means I'm already having a good time." I lean over and lower the volume of my voice. "But you definitely don't want to be the guy sitting by yourself, pining and drowning your sorrows in alcohol. You'll feel better if you're in the action, not watching it take place without you."

He takes another sip of champagne, polishing off the bottle before he nods, stands, and finally accepts my gesture.

I can feel Travis's eyes follow us as we hit the outer edge of the crowd, but I put all my energy into Nick.

"I'm actually kind of regretting this decision," I tell him as we watch the other couples.

He snorts. "Where's that bravado, Dakota? I just watched you chug a good amount of tequila solely to prove a point."

I shrug. "I use that superpower very sparingly. The bravado, that is. I have plenty of experience of sitting alone with nothing but my own mind to keep me company, but something tells me you don't. You seemed like you needed rescuing."

He sighs as he steps closer. "I guess we all need the occasional interference."

"I'm actually a horrible dancer." I grimace and cower just a little. "Clubs have never really been my thing."

"It's not about the dancing," Nick counters, pressing a hand to my lower back and pushing me into the crowd.

"What do you mean?" I ask hesitantly.

"I'm a musician. I live by the beat of the music. I can't

hear a song without some part of my body moving to the beat, whether it's tapping my feet or swaying my body as I'm playing."

"But you have a bass to keep your hands occupied," I point out, waving my hands awkwardly.

He smiles and spins me around so my back is flush against his chest. "Just find the rhythm, Dakota. Listen for the drum and move."

I attempt to dispel everything from my brain that's not Nick and the music playing—I really do try, but I can't do it. I'm too in my head, caught up with everyone around me, the vocals, the guitar, and everything I'm supposed to ignore.

I thought alcohol would loosen me up, but all the tequila I drank just makes me feel disoriented.

Nick chuckles, his breath hitting my back as he reaches around me and taps two fingers on my thigh in time with the beat.

"Now, move," he orders, moving his hand to my hip.

We bob back and forth for at least thirty seconds before we both break out into laughter at how uncoordinated I am, which works out just fine, giving us the release we both need.

"Thank you," he says.

I grin. "I'm glad my lack of rhythm could cheer you up."

He spins me around like we're slow dancing, and my gaze stops just over his shoulder, locking eyes with Travis.

"Let's try this again," Nick encourages.

"Okay," I say to him, to myself, to Travis, even though he can't hear me. "I'll do my best."

SIX

I don't have any scientific proof, facts, or any real reason to believe things have changed with Travis.

But I swear, I *feel* something has shifted between us.

It's kind of ridiculous, honestly, to cling to my intuition in this instance because all I'm doing is sitting in his trailer, but at least it's semi-comfortable silence.

In the car ride on the way here—because the label insisted I needed a private chauffeur to get to the set, which I honestly didn't hate—I watched a few behind-the-scenes videos of random music videos to get a feel for what to expect.

But even with that insight, it's generally less glamorous and more raw than I imagined.

I've been sitting in the same seat, just feet from Travis, watching as he gets doted on by professional stylists who tousle his hair with products and do endless touch-ups on his already flawless skin.

Part of me thinks they're doing it just to be close to him.

And frankly, I can't blame them.

At first, he's all smiles and chatty with everyone, including the producer who stops by to check in, but Travis's demeanor shifts after he gets a text message that apparently isn't pleasant.

I watch a little line of irritation form on his forehead as he spends a half hour rage-texting, and I use that time to speculate who the hell is on the other end.

"We're about twenty minutes out," the producer says, popping his head back in the trailer. "There's a delay with one of the lighting kits, and we're sorting it out."

"Thanks, man," Travis says, not lifting his eyes from the screen.

"We'll see you on set for touch-ups," one of the stylists says, unbuttoning the protective cape and putting it aside before they all follow the producer out.

Travis nods and shoves his phone in his pocket, then leans back in the chair, like the digital conversation has taken a lot out of him.

It's not a great sign, given that this shoot is going to be an all-day affair.

From what Leigh told me, the video is entirely Travis's vision. He's going to be in all sorts of different elements and settings, culminating into a big reveal at the end where he's having a quiet night in and writing in that damn black notebook.

I glance at his reflection in the mirror. "Travis."

"Dakota," he says evenly.

"Are you excited for the shoot?"

Surprisingly, he swivels his chair to face me full-on. "I am very excited to shoot the music video for 'Vantage Point,' the first single off my new album, *Honest Chaos*."

"Someone has been media-trained," I drawl, noting how he made a point to restate the question in his answer, which makes for a better quote.

"Just because I don't like interviews doesn't mean I'm not good at them."

I can't help but laugh at that. "I'd love to witness it in action, then. How about you answer a handful of questions for me?"

He squints at me, like he's trying to suss me out.

I rub my hands on my jean-clad thighs, glad I went for a more casual look today with sneakers after suffering through high heels last night.

"Tell me something," Travis says, knocking one of his knees against mine.

I'm a little off-put by the casual gesture, and I don't know if that was his intention, trying to soften me up. "What?"

I don't want to give up control of the interview—if I can even call this as much—but I wait him out, curious to see what he wants to know.

"What was that with Nick last night?" Travis asks evenly.

I blink. "I'm not sure what you mean."

"You do know he's not interested in you, right?"

"Travis," I say, more entertained than offended. "You don't really seem to have a lot of respect for reporters and the press, I get it. But do you really think I'm here to hook up with one of your bandmates? Even then, that I'd think he was sulking over Phoenix *just* because of their LP? Or I'm that naïve?"

He nods and exhales, seeming relieved. "You'd be surprised at the tactics people use to get an 'in' with me."

I do feel a little guilty at his statement.

Because although I'm not looking to get close to Travis for the reasons most people do, using Nick to do it did briefly cross my buzzed mind. Really, though, Nick is just a good guy stuck in a shitty situation, and if my volunteering to be his subpar dance partner made it even briefly better, it was worth it.

My breakup with Mark was frustrating enough, and we live almost four hundred miles apart—I can't imagine being in Nick's situation.

I frown at the thought. "I've just been there before," I say before I can second-guess my honesty. "It's been a while since I've been in a relationship, but I don't think anyone forgets the feeling of sitting on the sidelines and watching your ex move on. And how it hurts like hell, regardless of how much champagne is available to drown the sorrow."

Travis tilts his head, assessing my response.

"Ask me," he says finally, leaning back in his chair and propping his foot up on the wall.

"What?" I blurt out.

His blue eyes bore into mine. "Ask me your questions, Dakota."

I don't hesitate to act on the opening.

"Anything in particular you want to talk about?" I pose, swiping open the voice recording app on my phone.

"You're the journalist," he says petulantly.

"Tell me about your black notebook."

The corner of his mouth ticks up. "That wasn't a question."

I'm actually not annoyed by his quip, so I expand my query. "Most writers these days, myself included, tend to do everything digitally, but it appears you choose to put pen to paper. Why?"

"I've always done it this way," he says, tapping the front pocket of his jeans.

"When did you start writing?"

"High school English." His eyes drop momentarily, recalling the details. "Junior year. Fraley, right?"

"Oh, no, not Mr. Fraley," I groan, recalling his awful breath and grading style. "He was the absolute worst."

Travis smiles at me.

It's small, but it's there.

And I do my best to act like it doesn't make my heart sing.

"I forget exactly what the actual assignment was," he continues. "I'm pretty sure it was just straight-up journaling for a semester. All my friends thought it was a joke. They just jotted down garbage or drew dick pictures or whatever, but I loved it. Back then, I was so high and fucked up in the head that I had so much swirling around in my mind. Writing became an outlet for it all."

I nod in understanding. "And then, eventually, it became a habit?"

"Yeah. Who the hell knows how many notebooks I've filled since then, but I'm rarely, if ever, without one. Sometimes I write song lyrics. Sometimes I just take little notes that turn into them. And sometimes it's just a way to process my thoughts or pass the time."

I try to temper my excitement at these little bits of himself he's sharing with me. "Well then, I can certainly see the connection with the story you're telling with the video," I say, trying to segue into today's action.

He picks a nonexistent piece of lint from his shirt. "How so?"

"I thought I was the one asking the questions?" I tease, quirking an eyebrow. "But I guess since you answered one of mine, I can answer one of yours. This is without seeing the inspiration boards or the set, of course, but I've picked up enough that it seems like the different scenarios being staged are going to reflect everyone else's opinions of you. Or what your life seems like on the surface."

"Close," he admits.

I speculate further. "Or maybe it's a look back at your past, then that last scene with you writing it all down is just your way of showing how all your experiences funnel into your art. Is that more accurate?"

He shrugs. "I'll leave it up to your interpretation."

"Fair enough," I say. "So, what's the first thing—"

A knock sounds on the door before it opens.

"Travis, we're ready for you," the producer announces.

I think I see a flicker of disappointment on Travis's features, but he jumps up so quickly that I don't get to appreciate it fully.

When he lands lightly on his feet, he shakes out his shoulders like he's preparing to go out and challenge the world.

Maybe he is, in his own way.

I stop the voice recording on my phone, almost forgetting that was the purpose of our entire exchange.

Travis crosses the space with easy confidence, as usual, but it's almost ridiculous how he can even make his costume of khaki pants and a polo with a name tag on it actually look appealing.

"You coming?" he asks over his shoulder.

His words aren't exactly welcoming, but they're softer than they've been in our previous exchanges, and it feels like we've finally established some level of understanding with each other.

I smile at him, but just as I stand, my phone buzzes in my lap, flashing Mark's name and photo on the screen.

"I'll catch up," I promise Travis.

He nods, then bounds down the steps, letting the door slam shut behind him.

I clear my throat before I answer. "Mark. Hey."

"You don't sound happy to hear from the person who has news for you," he singsongs.

All the lightness I feel from my first real conversation with Travis dissipates. "Really?"

"Yep," he says proudly.

I run a hand through my hair. "Oh."

"Where are you right now? You're being oddly quiet."

"Sorry," I say with a wince. "I'm actually at a music video shoot. It's this all-day thing for his first single on the new album."

Mark chuckles. "Only you would be snippy about spending the day with all the glitz and the glamour and shit."

I don't bother correcting him or elaborating on why I

feel like I'm somehow betraying Travis because I, myself, don't understand it.

"No time for pleasantries and flirty banter, got it," he continues, thankfully. "Okay, apparently there was nothing nefarious about the split with his ex. Well, no more than you'd expect. She was dragging it out in hopes of getting more alimony, and eventually, it seems he gave in just to get it over with."

I chew on my thumbnail, hoping that's all he has for me. "Well, that's good for him, I guess."

"But not for your story," Mark says knowingly. "Which is why this next bit is worth your time."

I lean forward, more nervous to hear what's coming than I should be.

"Apparently, this one cop has it out for Travis. Has arrested him multiple times. And is sick of the guy's shit enough to convince the DA not to let him off easy, hence everything they're throwing at him, the extended probationary period, and that house arrest stint."

"That seems really excessive," I say, recalling everything I read in the court docket.

"Yep. I know you've seen the charges, and at least half of them are bogus. But there's a big final hearing coming up. It seems like Travis and his expensive lawyer are trying to put this shit behind them, but both the cop and the judge have warned him about being on his best behavior."

I try to process this information at rapid speed. "Well, his recent self-isolation makes sense, then. Do you think he's going to get cleared of the charges?"

"I'm not here to form opinions, Dakota. And you aren't either."

"Obviously." I roll my eyes. "But I better get going. Thanks for the information, Mark. It helps fill in some gaps on everything I'm finding out."

"Sure, sure," he says dismissively. "So when are you home next?"

"Oh," I breathe, hand on the trailer door. "I'm not sure."

"Well you definitely owe me a drink. Or many. If you're not doing anything for Thanksgiving, maybe I can come see you?"

Part of me aches for both of us, stuck in this situation where we've just dragged out whatever this has been between us. I don't want to hurt him anymore, but I don't know how to officially end this without doing just that.

Calling him was a mistake on so many levels.

"Maybe," I say half-heartedly. "I'll have to let you know."

"I understand." His tone is one of very clear disappointment. "You're busy."

"I am," I say, attempting to reassure him. "But at the very least, I should be home for Christmas this year."

"That's so far away."

I sigh. "I know, but hey, I've got to run. I'll...call you sometime soon, okay?"

"Take care of yourself, Dakota."

"For what it's worth, Mark, you're the best ex-boyfriend I've ever had," I say, then hang up and take a breath.

I try to push aside all my emotions and let myself be distracted with experiencing an entire day of Travis's perspective.

SEVEN

It takes me nearly the entire day to understand what Travis is *really* trying to say with the music video.

The entire setup is in front of a green screen, which apparently will help them shoot and release the video faster. There are limited props and set pieces, but I can still picture it just fine—even if my eyes are a little strained from the bright shade of the backdrop.

From what I can tell, my earlier suspicions were correct, and all the scenes seem somewhat autobiographical.

Travis is clearly the star of the video, as he should be, but Nick and Phoenix also appear in the different scenarios with him, even though they weren't with him in the beginning of his career.

The first shot of the day shows the group working at a fast-food joint, then playing shows with only a handful of people in the audience before it switches to what appears to be a house party.

It's interesting to see how Travis commands the shoot

in tandem with the director, giving suggestions to the extras on how to act in scenes, even pulling in one of the stylists to make tweaks to some of their outfits and hairstyles.

I'm fascinated by the entire ordeal and coordination of it all that I don't even get to appreciate Travis's performing chops until he belts out the chorus directly down the camera.

I wanna tell you it's all going to be fine, be fine
But all I can do is just hold on, hold on
My vantage point is exposure, composure
Until the cuffs get handed over
Then it's isolation without sedation
Pressure and persuasion
Be fine, be fine, hold on, hold on

There's a backtrack that guides them, but they perform as if it doesn't exist.

Phoenix absolutely crushes it on drums, using his entire body to support the movement of his sticks on the entire kit. His head bobs to the beat before he grins at Nick, the most tense out of the trio, as he strums his fingers.

But it's Travis who commands the attention of nearly everyone around me—the director, the producers, the extras, and the record label executives who just arrived.

He uses a fretless electric guitar, something I have to look up when someone mentions it offhand, but I quickly learn it's the source of what makes this album so distinctive and alluring to me.

The sound is a little distorted, but that somehow heightens the listening and viewing experience.

He croons into the microphone, spending most of the chorus with intense eyes, like he's begging the audience for something, and I'm helpless to do anything other than sit still and take it all in.

As everyone breaks, finally, I get in line for lunch and notice Travis, Phoenix, and Nick don't join the crew, instead heading over to Travis's trailer. And Devin, along with a few female models from the party scene and a bottle of vodka, sneaks off from the set.

"Dakota," Leigh calls to me. "Join us."

I smile as I take a seat beside her. "Thanks."

She waves a hand to the table. "You can ask anyone here any question you want."

"Well, maybe not *anything* you want," one of the guys jokes.

"Great," I say, ignoring the grumbling of my stomach as I set my phone on the table to record our conversation.

"Let me officially introduce you to Jamie from marketing and Drew, the head of distribution." Leigh gestures to each person with her fork in a sort of stabbing motion. "They've both been with Travis since he signed on with the label."

I nod. "So you've seen firsthand how he's grown as an artist?"

One of the most important yet basic skills I learned in journalism school is to prompt and then shut the hell up.

I rarely watch interviews on television because it grates on me when the hosts insert themselves into the conversation, regaling the audience with anecdotes about their own lives.

As a journalist, it's fair to say that I'm less interesting to my readers than the subject I'm covering. My job is to simply tell the story.

And it's clear to me that Jamie and Drew are both pros at navigating discourse like this as they give me optimal quotes off the cuff and soundbites with only the slightest nudge.

"What has that been like?" I ask them both at once.

"From the first meeting with Travis, I knew he was something special," Drew answers. "Not because of his raw talent, although there is plenty of it, but because of his *vision* for everything from guitar riffs, lyrics, and melodies to the color of his shoelaces on the album covers."

Jamie nods along before adding her own perspective. "Travis Young is a new kind of performer, refusing to stay stagnant in his genre. He's not afraid to push the boundaries of who he is as a musician and an artist, and we're all benefiting from it."

"Has that ever been more true than with *Honest Chaos*?" I ask.

"The latest record is, without a doubt, his best yet," Jamie gushes. "Fans should be ready for a roller coaster of realness in Travis's writing."

It continues on like that until it's time for lunch to wrap, timing perfectly with my phone notifying me that the battery is low.

I thank Jamie and Drew for their time, glad to have some quotes, even if they are pretty biased.

I excuse myself from the group and walk back to

Travis's trailer, intending on grabbing my portable charger from my purse, but I'm stopped short by the sound of arguing.

"Are you fucking *kidding* me?" Travis's voice is the angriest I've ever heard it.

I turn the corner to see him and the director facing off against Devin and his entourage of women, who are swaying in their high heels.

"We're just having a little fun, bro," Devin slurs. "Lighten up. It's a music video with a party scene."

Travis's jaw clenches. "The *party* is over."

"Come on, Trav."

Travis's chest heaves, and it's not just frustration I sense but something deeper—hurt, maybe.

"Get out of my sight," he snaps.

Thankfully, Devin obliges, taking the gaggle of tall, long-legged ladies with him.

"Fuck," Travis breathes, running a hand through his hair.

The director takes off his hat and sighs. "We could probably make do with what we have so far. Maybe record a few more shots of you guys playing and then cut in different backgrounds."

"It's not what we talked about, though." Travis frowns, obviously upset at the possibility of having to compromise his vision. "Doesn't it feel like an incomplete story? Like all I've been striving for is to just go from a deadbeat piece of shit to a rockstar?"

"I can make some calls and see if we can get anyone in here today, but it's a tight turnaround," the director says. "Maybe we can see if the space is available tomorrow?"

Travis shakes his head. "The label threw a fit about this concept already. They wanted to hire actors and do something simple and artsy. If we have to bleed into tomorrow, it's going to cost, like, thirty grand. I doubt they'll be willing to pay."

"Shit," the director says on an exhale.

Even as I'm listening, I realize I *really* shouldn't be eavesdropping like this, though it's nothing of major consequence.

Still, I don't want to be seen as someone trying to benefit from their bad situation, hoping to turn it into some sort of point in the story.

"Excuse me," I say, outing myself as I attempt to slide past them toward the trailer.

"Wait," the director demands. "Who are you?"

"I'm just passing through."

He steps in my path and eyes me up and down. "Hold on."

I hold my hands up defensively. "No one you need to worry about," I say quickly. "I'm just going to grab my—"

"What do you think?" He ignores my deflection and directs his question to Travis.

Travis blinks and takes a step back, like he's regarding me from a new perspective.

"No way," I start, already seeing the plan formulating in his mind. "No fucking way."

"Instead of using a different model for every setup, we can blur her in and out, change her outfits," the director poses. "It might actually make more sense for the story, if you think about it."

"What about Leigh?" I suggest a little desperately. "Jamie from marketing?"

"She's right for the look," he continues. "She's got the right height paired with you, and just imagine the contrast between your jet-black hair and her blonde hair."

I swallow, then chew on my bottom lip.

"Dakota," Travis says evenly.

Before he even asks, I already know I'm going to agree.

Not only will it earn me major bonus points with him but I can already imagine Bryan salivating at the narrative I'll tell when I work it into the story.

"That's not a question," I deadpan, throwing his earlier deflection back at him.

He takes a deep breath. "Dakota, will you do this for me?"

"Say please," I retort, smile tugging at the corner of my mouth.

The director bursts out laughing. "She *is* perfect for this."

"Dakota Shaw, will you please do me a favor and stand around looking pretty on camera?"

The hidden compliment is jarring, but I don't flinch.

"Fine," I agree.

"Good." The director rubs his hands together. "Then let's get to it. We don't have a lot of time."

They usher me back to Travis's trailer, and within minutes, I go from normalcy to full glamour mode as the stylists descend upon me, leaving me coughing at the obscene amount of product used to keep my now slightly wavy curls intact.

I watch with some amusement as clothes are pulled

frantically from their hangers, glad it's not my job to figure out how to adjust ensembles that were intended for women three inches taller and twenty pounds lighter than me.

Less than an hour after I agreed to this insanity, I step out of the trailer in sky-high heels and a bright blue party dress—neither of which I'd ever wear in my regular life.

The director lets me grip his forearm as we walk to the set, and he gives me a rundown of the three scenes I'll be in. The first isn't that much different from the setup I saw before lunch, but as the song mellows out post-chorus, the spotlights will just be on Travis and me, indicating that he's found a connection with someone.

I nod along as he dives into the details of camera angles, then tells me I just have to stand there with a "look of intense passion" on my face.

He harps on it enough that as I cross in front of the camera, I'm actually a little nervous I'm going to mess it all up.

As I stand on the mark about ten feet away from Travis, our eyes lock, and he immediately shakes his head.

"No," Travis says abruptly. "It's too much."

"Too much what?" the director asks, waving the makeup artist over.

"Everything. She's naturally gorgeous, and you pretty much painted a new face for her."

I blink. "Thank you."

"You're welcome," Travis says like it's no big deal.

"But do I need to be recognizable?" I ask. "Isn't this pretend?"

He softens. "I just want it to feel genuine."

"Okay," I say, understanding that.

I wipe off the ruby red lipstick with the back of my hand, earning a gasp from the makeup artist, and I can practically *feel* the glare from the stylist as I kick off the uncomfortable shoes.

Travis steps toward me and slips off his sleek black leather jacket—the one he eyed in the boutique—for me to put on.

"No," the director snaps. "Save that for when we're rolling."

Travis obliges, then picks up his guitar and waves for us to get started.

The scene goes by quickly, and to the director's credit, he was right about me mostly just standing there as Travis shreds on his guitar and sings to me.

From my vantage point, I see the truth
But I hope someone will save me
Maybe an angel like you

My hands shake as the cameraman moves the setup closer, capturing the little details as Travis puts his jacket around my shoulders.

It takes some time to adjust to the spotlight and the number of people staring, but after the fifth take, I relax.

The second shot is supposed to be our wedding, and we're apparently going to do a trick shot where the camera pans to Travis in his performing clothes, then to me in a wedding dress, then back to him but in a tuxedo.

I nearly faint at the sight of Travis in such a formal look with his hair slicked back, and judging by the way Leigh and Jamie giggle from the sidelines, I'm not the only one who feels that way.

The dress I'm wearing wouldn't be my first choice. It's a little ostentatious, adorned with jewels and a full skirt, but I get the look we're going for here.

And most importantly, it looks fantastic on camera.

When we finish that scene, we slip into more casual clothes, thankfully, consisting of matching black hoodies, jeans, and the shoes he just launched. The crew wheels in an oversized and very comfortable couch for the final shot.

Travis falls casually on the leather cushions and gestures for me to come join him while the crew adjusts the lighting. A muted TV plays Travis's other videos and clips of him on the red carpet, and I'm trying to pinpoint the direct message he's trying to get across.

"Is this what you really want?" I ask him quietly as people flitter around us. "To settle down and get married?"

"It's not necessarily a goal, but I think it could be part of the plan," he admits quietly, fiddling with the rings on his fingers. "You know how you were asking the meaning behind the video?"

I nod. "Uh-huh."

"I just want a simple life, Dakota. I do want to write and perform, and I enjoy being an artist, but if there's anything I've learned in the past few years, it's that all this shit, the money, the private jets, the parties...it's all superficial. And I'm ready to dig a little deeper."

"That makes sense," I say dumbly, a little awed by his declaration.

He pulls out his notebook and runs his thumb along the spine of it. "It's the truth."

"Ready?" the director asks us.

We both nod as the playback starts up.

"Get all cozy and content," he orders. "You're supposed to be in love. Whatever the hell that means."

Travis and I both smirk, then he tosses an arm around the back of the couch, and I move a little closer to him.

"In *love*," the director repeats.

Travis rolls his eyes and scoops me up in his arms, settling me on his lap.

My breathing is loud in my ears, but I try to calm myself as the song decrescendos.

As I relax into Travis's hold, he opens his notebook and writes words that only I get to see.

Is Dakota a state of mind?
Or a ghost in the present tense?

And I can't help but wonder if, in this proximity, he can feel my heart pounding in my chest.

EIGHT

I decide to reward myself for a job well done at the shoot yesterday by skipping out on the meetings that are on this morning's agenda.

I don't need any more context of his relationship with the label and what they think of him—or at least, what they *say* they think of him.

Because I've picked up on enough tenseness and snarky comments between Travis and the label that it's clear that the relationship isn't the easiest.

Still, I give Leigh a heads-up, saying I need to get some stuff done and won't be in attendance, and she doesn't push the issue.

What I do actually need is time to sort out everything I know about Travis Young before our final meeting tomorrow afternoon. If he doesn't sit down with me for an *actual* interview, this story is going to be complete shit.

I get organized on the sofa in my apartment—computer

fully charged, music on low volume, snacks and water within arm's reach—and get ready to let it all pour out.

But just as I bring my fingers to my keyboard, my phone buzzes.

"Mom," I answer on the first ring. "Is everything okay?"

"Why do you always assume something is wrong when I call?" she asks innocently.

"Because there usually is," I remind her. "Some sort of crisis with the book club or Dad or an argument with Aunt Helene."

She snorts into the receiver. "Well, imagine this...I just wanted to call and see how my favorite and only daughter is faring in big, beautiful New York City. It's been *days* since I've heard from you."

"I know."

"Not even one measly text for your mother."

"I've been on an assignment."

Even I know that's kind of a lame excuse, given that I'm rarely more than three feet away from my phone, but it's the truth.

"Taking down another scummy rich guy?" she asks. "Or another one of those reports on climate change?"

"No, actually, this is different from anything I've ever done before."

That surprises her. "Really?"

"Do you remember Travis Young?" I ask tentatively.

She pauses. "Wasn't he a speaker at your high school graduation?"

"No," I say with a chuckle. "Pretty much the exact opposite. He's a famous singer now."

"The guy with all the tattoos? And that eyebrow piercing?"

I lean back into the couch cushions. "That's the one."

"Oh, I *like* him," she gushes.

"Mom!"

She laughs. "What? Your mother can't think someone is attractive? I'm old, not without taste."

"Don't objectify the subject of my next story, Mom," I whine.

"*You* are writing about him?"

"My editor made me." It's the simplest explanation I can come up with. "Uh, I should probably warn you that I'm also going to be in his next music video."

"What?" she gasps. "This is all so exciting! How did this even happen?"

I fill her in on all the details so far, and she presses for more information and continues to shriek in delight.

"The book club girls are going to be *so* jealous," my mom says happily. "Connie was just going on and on last week about how her daughter got invited backstage at some stupid concert, but this is way better."

"Well, glad I could help," I say sourly.

"Hush. When are you coming home?"

"I don't know. Maybe before Christmas, depending on the story I cover next."

"You work too hard," my mom chides me like she always does. "You need to take a break every once in a while."

"I know."

"Dakota Jane."

I sigh. "I'll try, Mom."

"That's all I ask," she says. "I love you. Call me soon."

"Love you, too," I return before ending the call.

Despite her pleading, I don't take a break.

I spend the rest of the day putting together the framework of my piece, inserting chunks of interview and trying to intersperse it with narrative, but it still feels so incomplete. The little snippets of conversation with Travis aren't nearly enough, and the quotes from the record label executives are so laughably slanted that it pains me to have nothing else to balance them out.

I open a new document to start jotting down a running list of questions for Travis and decide I'm going to try and sit down with Phoenix and Nick, too. Although they weren't with him from the very beginning, they likely have more insight into him than anyone else.

And that thought irks me slightly.

Because out of all the photographs I've seen of him and the time I've spent with him, I'm curious as to whom he confides in. His bandmates seem to have their own drama, and his brother...well, even if I hadn't seen their exchange yesterday, I would know there's definitely something troubling brewing there. On top of that, Travis hasn't been photographed with anyone romantically for at least four years.

So who sees the real him?

Does anyone?

And what do *I* even really know about him?

Other than the fact he's a globe-traveling rockstar with killer blue eyes and a little black notebook...not much at all.

That realization dampens my mood so severely that I'm still trying to shake it the next day.

I'm slightly appeased by the ability to fall right back into my normal routine—coffee, prep, the right timing for the train commute in, arriving to my desk while it's still quiet.

"Hey, Dakota," Christina says, smiling brightly. "How's it going?"

"Just fine, thanks," I reply curtly. "How are you?"

"Good. But I *have* to fill you in on what happened with Ryan after you left the other night. He got really drunk and started telling me about all the drama in the sales department."

She moves to sit down on my desk, and I frown inwardly, not really interested in whatever workplace shenanigans another department has gotten into. It's not just because I'm feeling iffy about her over our failed night out, but my mind is elsewhere.

"Dakota," Bryan greets as he crosses the threshold of the newsroom. "Let's meet first thing."

Christina pouts. "But I need an update on how everything is going with Travis Young," she says, all smiles again. "Lunch today?"

"Probably not," I say as I stand to head to Bryan's office.

She frowns for real this time. "Oh."

"Maybe once things settle down?" I offer, not wanting to sever things entirely.

"Okay," she agrees, sounding marginally more cheerful.

Once I step inside Bryan's office, he orders, "Shut the door."

I quirk an eyebrow, surprised by his off-the-bat brashness. "Okay," I say, obliging him before I take a seat. "What's up?"

"Do you want the good news first or the bad?"

I hate when people ask that question instead of just delivering the information, but since he's already in a mood, I don't express my opinion on the matter.

"Bad," I answer.

He cracks open a Diet Coke. "Ellison Incorporated is suing us for libel," he says evenly.

I roll my eyes as he takes a sip. "We both know that's a farce."

Libel cases are nearly impossible to win, not to mention we have public records and sources to back up our claims. And also, the fact that Roger Ellison is a public figure makes it even more far-fetched.

They're likely suing just to take a public stand, irritate *Exos*, and make an example out of us as a warning for any other publication considering picking up the story.

"Of course it is." Bryan nods, then sighs. "But that doesn't mean it's not a pain in the ass or a massive expense. It's going to drain our legal team of resources to take the case far enough in the process to get it thrown out."

"Why do I feel like you're more worried about this than you should be?" I ask tentatively.

"Because I know that after you finish the Travis Young piece you have a mile-long wish list of other articles you want to write related to this story."

I lace my fingers together on my lap. "Yes. And?"

"Ownership doesn't want you to touch anything

connected to this for the time being," Bryan tells me with a wince.

"What?" I demand. "You've got to be kidding me."

"Afraid not, Dakota." He pauses and taps on the side of the can. "But this does bring me to my good news."

"You're telling me there's something good coming out of me getting sidelined after reporting a *fair* and very *accurate* story?" I retort, completely exasperated.

He ignores my attitude as he clicks a few buttons on his computer. "The label executives at the video shoot got an idea when you did your little cameo. Thanks for telling me about that, by the way."

I grimace. "Sorry."

"They don't just want a story with photos anymore," Bryan explains.

"Well, good thing we don't let *them* decide our editorial vision…"

He leans forward, placing his elbows on the desk. "They're asking if we'd be interested in doing a mini documentary, like the one the features team did last fall with that teen actress."

Normally, the feature stories aren't even on my radar, but for months, upper management at *Exos* kept congratulating the team on the well-produced video.

I'm sure they were mostly excited about all the sponsors dying to be a part of it—and for good reason. Last I checked, the forty-minute piece had more than twenty million views.

"This will certainly offset legal costs related to Ellison Incorporated," I piece together out loud.

"And *that's* why you're my senior reporter." Bryan smiles. "Once you sign the paperwork, we're all set."

"Travis is on board with this?" I ask, a little surprised.

"It's not really his call, but from what I hear, yes. They're trying to give a behind-the-scenes look at the direction shift and give a little context and realness behind the music."

"When did all this happen?"

"I got the phone call last night and the confirmation paperwork in my inbox first thing this morning."

I run a hand through my hair, unsure how I'm even really feeling about this, but I don't think it matters.

"I don't really have a choice, do I?"

"This is going to be huge, Dakota," Bryan presses, a little irritated. "Not only is it going to be great for *Exos* but it's probably going to elevate your career to the next level."

My mind is reeling. "How so?"

He turns his computer toward me and zooms in on one of the pages.

I squint as I read the fine print detailing the parties responsible and tossing around legal jargon until my eyes land on my own name.

"Dakota Shaw, executive producer," I recite aloud. "Are you serious?"

He nods. "Read the next line."

I can feel my eyes almost bug out of my head at the salary details. "I'm going to get paid *extra* to do my job?"

"Yep," he says smugly.

"This sounds too good to be true, Bryan. What's the catch?"

"Weeks of living and breathing Travis Young. You're

going to be 'on' practically all day and night, traveling on the first leg of his tour in the U.S., then you'll fly back here and live in the edit room until it comes out. We're on an extremely tight turnaround, and both the opportunity and pressure of this are unreal."

Those words might frighten some, but I can't back down from the challenge.

I mull it over, picture embedding myself in this lifestyle for two months and having more repeats of yesterday, and damn if I'm not intrigued.

When I meet Bryan's gaze after a beat, I realize how wide his smile is.

I narrow my eyes. "What do you get from this?"

Bryan and I have been through a lot—arguments with each other and upper management and a hell of a lot of late nights—but he's just as much a protector from the establishment as he is an enabler of it.

He wouldn't be pushing his senior reporter away for two months if he wasn't getting something in return.

"I'm up for editor-in-chief next year with Craig retiring," he admits, unable to suppress a smile.

I can't even be annoyed that he's using me to leverage his promotion because of how awesome that would be for him.

"Holy shit," I exclaim. "That's great, Bryan! It's about time."

He nods in agreement. "Couldn't have done it without you, Dakota."

"That's not true," I say honestly. "But I appreciate the sentiment."

"Well, anyway, you and I have to head upstairs to meet

the legal team at eleven to sign the papers, and then we'll receive the official tour schedule and details."

"Sounds good," I say, standing up at his dismissal.

"Dakota?" he calls before I leave. "I know how you're going to approach this assignment, but please do try and enjoy it. I can think of a worse way to pass the time than schmoozing and partying with the rich and famous."

And I actually kind of agree.

NINE

Leigh is my new best friend.

Or at least, you'd think she was, given how much we've texted back and forth in the days leading up to the official launch of the tour.

The good news is that I'm excused from more mind-numbing meetings with the label under the guise of preparing for going on the road and filming.

In that time, I meet Dan, *Exos*'s resident videographer who is going to be along for the ride with me.

I bring him up to speed, giving him the rundown of what I know about Travis Young, and walking him through my notes and some of the highlights from the research I've conducted—although I don't share the information I got from Mark just yet—then we listen to the interviews I've gathered so far.

Bryan joins us for an all-day planning session, and we create a very rough frame of the story we'll tell about

Travis, planning interview slots and noting what concert venues might bring about the best footage.

Of course, we can't really know what the narrative will be or what scenes we'll include until we get a feel for what it's like.

I would think that would be an issue, given the time and effort we're putting into it, but Bryan implies that we could just put forty minutes of Travis signing autographs while shirtless and viewers would be happy.

Christina is living proof of his claim.

She is ridiculously jealous of the opportunity I have, and she isn't shy about letting me know. Her envy is interspersed with moments of wondering out loud if she can cover my beat in my absence.

I do my best to ignore her and focus on the fact I'm going to be giving a rock band my full attention for the next eight weeks.

As Dan and I finalize our checklist for equipment and packing, Leigh calls me for the umpteenth time.

"You sure you don't want to come backstage or to the rehearsal for tonight?" she asks as soon as I answer.

"Totally certain," I say.

"But it's Madison Square Garden," she reminds me. "The world's most famous arena and all that."

I chuckle. "I know. Dan will definitely take advantage of his press badge, so he has free rein, but I'm going to watch the concert for the first time like any other attendee."

"If you're sure," she says, not totally convinced.

"Yep."

To be fair, Bryan doesn't agree with my plan either, but

he has bigger things to worry about than where I'm sitting at a concert.

I just think it's important to have a blank slate and get a dose of perspective before I'm tossed in the whole behind-the-scenes world of music production and touring.

It might not make a huge difference, but it feels like the right thing to do.

"Okay," Leigh relents. "If I don't talk to you again tonight, just remember that the car will collect you at eight tomorrow morning."

"I'll be ready," I promise, thinking of the clothes already packed in my suitcases. "Thank you."

"And text me if you have trouble getting into the show," she adds. "Bye!"

Thankfully, we don't have any hiccups while making our way to the iconic arena.

Dan and I pick up our tickets at will call, and we go through security just like everyone else. He already has his camera out, filming the procession of people as we move past the merchandise tables and up the escalators.

The excitement is palpable, and I'm a little surprised by the wide variety of ages in attendance, seeing just as many couples in their forties as I do groups of teens.

I think back to my first concert, a small indie rock show that a friend in high school dragged me to.

We thought we were so cool for wearing low-rise jeans and shirts that exposed our belly buttons. I vividly recall that the venue smelled like stale beer and peanuts, and I spent the whole concert trying not to get sensory overload.

Madison Square Garden, however, is about as different from that as I can get.

For as long as I've lived in New York, I've never actually attended a basketball game or a concert, but I appreciate it as an institution in the city. So many legends have wandered the halls and played here, which is why Leigh hoped we'd want to document it as part of our story.

But the angle Dan and I want to take is more about Travis as a person, so although this is part of his journey, it's not crucial to the story.

I wanted the normal concert-goer point of view, but the usher leads us past the crowded floor to a boxed-off section just behind the press area.

It makes sense, I guess, given that Dan does want to get a few shots, but it's almost uncomfortable to be this close to the stage.

The warm-up band, a small act also signed to the label, starts their set, and part of me considers the real possibility that my eardrums won't survive this tour.

Dan bobs his head along to the beat of the most popular song, and I count down the minutes until Travis is supposed to take the stage.

They take a bow, finishing their set, and immediately the crew starts to set up for Travis and the guys. I try to log all the faces that cross the stage.

I learned from Leigh that there are actually two identical sets of equipment and two teams contracted for the tour—one sets up the current day's event and is in charge of seeing it through, while the other is en route to ready the next.

I jot down notes on my phone, cataloging everything I've observed so far to be reminded of the first night feels when we eventually sit down to cut this thing together.

The lights in the arena dim, interrupting my train of thought, and the crowd of thousands wails in excitement.

Even though I can't see him, I know it's Travis who almost gently strums on his guitar, kicking off the set with the first song on their new album.

Around the stage, light bulbs slowly warm up, framing the trio as Travis approaches the microphone, singing the first lines of "Honest Chaos," the title track.

I will not stop
I will not stop
Until we can go
Go, go, go

He barely finishes the first lines before another round of enthusiastic screams erupts from the audience, and the roar only grows as Phoenix lets the drums kick in and Travis and Nick thrash on stage.

Travis can't help but smile at the energy before throwing his guitar around his back and gripping the microphone with both hands.

It's time for reflection
And self-deprecation
So fuck the albatross
I'm here for the honest chaos

"This is fucking amazing," Dan screams beside me, panning the camera, to take in the scene around us.

I crane my neck to see that even the people with seats

up in the highest part of the balcony are on their feet, screaming and dancing.

I will not stop
I will not stop
I will not stop
Until we can go
Back to the top

As the song winds down, Travis puts the microphone back on the stand and runs his hands through his hair.

"New York City!" he bellows over the whooping and chatter. "We hope you enjoy tonight. We love you!"

Phoenix taps his drumsticks together three times, then they dive into the next song.

The concert continues on, and the momentum, some-how, increases.

I watch, slightly awed, as the band members coordinate their movements and give the crowd their all for each song, moving constantly as they perform.

I'm glad I got the opportunity to listen to the record on my own because seeing it in person is completely different and even better than I envisioned.

Halfway through their set, I catch Nick's gaze.

He grins at me before swaying his hips to the beat of the drums, just like we did that night on the dancefloor, and I mimic his movements until I burst into laughter.

As one song comes to an abrupt end, Travis picks at chords that sound too familiar to me at this point.

"So, the other day, we filmed the music video for this song," Travis says into the mic as the crowd screams in excitement. "And I was asked about the meaning of it all. Not just the song but the story I want to tell visually with it."

My breath hitches.

"I have my own thoughts and interpretations, just like you will, but I hope what you all will take away from this is that the dreams that you want *can* be your reality. What you want isn't just a state of mind. It's a destination. Put yourself on the path and go for it."

I let the smile spread on my face, not realizing until after I release the emotion that Dan has the camera pointed at me.

"Stop," I say, rolling my eyes and shoving it out of my face. "I'm not the story. He is."

I point to Travis.

Dan shrugs as he turns back to the stage, capturing as much detail as he can.

And I'm left grappling with the thought of when, if ever, I'll get used to this.

TEN

I've always hated flying.

When I was a kid, my parents took me on a trip to Disney World for my thirteenth birthday, and we had enough turbulence on that flight to leave a lasting impression on me for the years that followed.

As an adult now, when I visit my hometown, I choose to make the long drive across Pennsylvania in a rental car rather than sit on a plane for a little more than an hour. I know it's not efficient, but it's my preference.

But I suppose even I, with my fried nerves, can see the appeal of flying on a private jet.

The black car drops me and my luggage off at a terminal that's so off the radar, it's not even on those big, directional signs.

From there, I'm ushered through the smallest security area I've ever seen—seriously, even the setup at Madison Square Garden seemed more intense—until I finally meet Leigh in a private suite to wait for our time to board.

"I wish we had time to get massages," she says with a frown, looking at the menu of services a little sadly. "But the car should be here shortly to take us out on the tarmac."

I already know this is the first of many wealth gaps I'll experience on this assignment, and judging by Dan's shocked expression as a man in a suit brings him in to join us, he's feeling the same way.

"They'll serve food and drinks on the plane," Leigh explains. "But feel free to stock up with what you want."

She gestures to an impressive array of snacks and bottled beer and wine, but I'm too nervous for the impending flight to take anything.

It's also a general rule that, as a reporter, you shouldn't take any handouts from your sources—although, I've already kind of learned that the rules don't apply for this story.

Dan, however, has no trouble raiding the spread before we are led to a BMW that shuttles us around the airport and past the runways until we pull up to the plane.

At least, I'm told it's a real plane, but to my eyes, it looks like a toy.

The exterior is *tiny* compared to my memories of the craft I flew in to and from Orlando all those years ago, but the inside is actually kind of spacious, with at least a dozen seating options.

"Welcome," a smiling flight attendant says. "Please take a seat, any place you'd like, and get buckled in. We'll be departing as soon as the others arrive."

I nod and head directly to the back where the window shades are pulled down.

Somehow, I think I'll feel better if I can't actually see us rise up into the air.

Leigh and Dan settle in beside each other on the U-shaped couch in the middle of the plane. It looks far cozier than my seat at a table, but I feel more secure with something to grip in my hands.

I sigh and sink back against the leather as Travis, Phoenix, Nick, Devin, and two crew members I recognize from the show last night finally come onboard.

"Hey, guys, this is Dan," Leigh says like she's showing off a prize.

My colleague stands, and they all do that half-handshake, half-hug thing before he's immediately brought into the fold of their conversation.

Jealousy surfaces at the way he easily assimilates into the group, but maybe it's not a bad thing that they hit it off right away.

Moments later, the flight attendant brings out a tray of mimosas in champagne glasses, which I politely decline in favor of wringing my hands. I'm the only one who doesn't indulge.

Dan, with his camera in one hand and the glass in the other, focuses his lens on the cheers-ing that takes place, and then everyone is encouraged to take their seats.

After attentively watching the safety demonstrations, we're officially on our way.

I close my eyes as we lurch forward.

My mind cycles through all the plane crashes I've read about in news stories—the accompanying photos always show the blackened metal and twisted remnants of the engine and exterior parts that survived the flames.

I should have read up on the safety statistics of flying commercial versus private and planned accordingly.

Like what if I've made a grave mistake by sitting in the back?

That thought makes my stomach drop.

"You okay?" Travis asks as he takes the seat beside me.

I take a few steadying breaths as he buckles in and kicks his feet up on the cushion across from us.

He's the pinnacle of a relaxed rockstar, sipping his drink and looking right at home, whereas I'm a nervous wreck.

I don't have time to question his motive or interest in sitting beside me because the plane starts moving faster, and I have to dig my nails into the hard surface of the table to keep my cool.

Travis's eyes take in my posture. "I take it you don't like flying?"

"That obvious?" I bite out.

"Here." He drops a Tootsie Roll Pop, encased in a dark blue wrapper, on the table. "This will help."

I give him a disbelieving gaze as the plane picks up speed. "How is the absolute worst flavor of a Tootsie Pop going to help this situation?"

"Are you kidding me? The *worst*?"

"Chocolate is the best," I insist.

"You're so wrong," Travis disagrees.

"Almost every flavor is better than grape. I mean, it's just artificial. No grape I've ever eaten in my life tastes like that."

"And yet, when you have something grape-flavored, you immediately know what it is."

I feel the moment the plane leaves the earth, and my stomach clenches.

"Did you ever go to the community pool growing up?" Travis asks, distracting me with his question.

I shake my head. "No. I'm not much of a swimmer."

"Well, I spent, like, every summer there as a kid. Was even a lifeguard there before junior year. And Tootsie Pops were only ten cents each."

"And you've had them in your pockets ever since?"

"Nah," he breathes. "Phoenix wanted to stop at a bodega for cigarettes before we boarded, and I impulse-bought one at the counter."

I nod. "Nostalgia's a bitch."

"That's actually not a bad song name," Travis jokes.

"Yeah, well, I am a *writer*," I remind him, immediately regretting the insinuation that he, in fact, is not. "Although, that is definitely your area of expertise."

He snorts. "I'll leave the investigative reporting to you."

"I am impressed by your style, though," I admit.

His head tilts to the side. "What do you mean?"

"I've considered myself a professional storyteller for almost ten years. I've probably published hundreds of articles and can't even begin to imagine what my word count is. But when I listen to your songs..." I trail off.

"When you listen to my songs?" Travis prompts.

I swallow and lower my voice. "It's like a punch to the gut in the best way possible."

His brow furrows, then he lets out a chuckle. "Well, that's certainly an interesting review."

"It's admirable, really, to tell a story that flows that well in such a short timeframe," I babble as the plane continues its ascent. "It's like how I've always loved and appreciated poetry, but my brain doesn't work in a way that would let me write it. You can tell a story in two lines that would take me several pages and annotations to explain."

"I appreciate the compliment," he says. "But I think it's just different training. You went to college and had time and resources to break down literary techniques and shit. I stood at the grill of a taco shop and tried to get words down in my notebook between customers."

Out of everything I considered Travis Young and I could possibly argue about, I would have never guessed it would be lollipop flavors or trying to accept compliments from each other.

"But then I just publish my words alongside photos that someone else has taken," I press. "You take your words and build all these sounds around them, which heightens the emotion being evoked. And not to mention that actually playing music is a completely different art."

A *pop!* interrupts me and startles me so wholly that if I wasn't buckled in, I would hit the ceiling of the plane with how forcefully I jump.

My gaze snaps to the direction of the sound, and I exhale as I watch Devin attempt to suck down the bubbles from the freshly opened champagne bottle.

Travis laughs beside me, and as I turn to glare at him, I realize that Dan has the camera pointed at us.

I sink back into the seat and frown.

I don't know how much audio he picked up from that distance or over the sound of the recycled air being pumped through the cabin, but I'm uncomfortable with the idea of this somewhat private conversation being recorded.

Which is a very, very bad thing for a journalist to think while speaking to a source.

"Is this what you normally do on planes?" I ask Travis. "Party like you do on the ground?"

He glances at Devin, who is animatedly chatting with Phoenix while holding the bottle in his hand.

"Usually I'll do some writing, listen to music, watch a movie, or catch up on sleep. Maybe all those things today, since it's a long flight."

"Makes sense," I say.

As the plane levels out, the flight attendant moves among us, collecting discarded glasses and offering clean ones along with more orange juice if needed.

"Do you want to watch something?" Travis asks.

I shake my head. "I'm good."

I kick my feet up, just like he has, and try to loosen up, but it doesn't have the intended effect. As I relax further, exhaustion hits me all at once—my long days at the *Exos* office, the late night after the concert last night, the fear of flying, the banter.

It's shameful how tired I am on the first day of the tour.

I barely cover my yawn as it surfaces.

"Maybe you'll sleep first, then watch something," Travis muses before waving the attendant over to us. "Can we get a blanket and a pillow, please?"

"Of course, Mr. Young," she says with a smile.

I glance over at him. "You didn't have to do that."

"Who says they're for you?" Travis jokes.

I roll my eyes as the woman returns, handing him the bundle that he immediately drops on my lap.

"Thank you," I murmur, unrolling the blanket to cover my lower half and settling in.

He nods and stands up, tapping on the seat behind my head before crossing the aisle to sit beside Devin.

I stare at the Tootsie Pop he left on the table, the sugary sweet, figurative olive branch.

Before I can overthink it, I stuff it in my purse, then get comfortable enough to let the drone of the others' conversations lull me to sleep.

ELEVEN

One perk of flying directly from New York to Los Angeles is that the guys get an extra three hours of downtime before the first of their back-to-back performances in the city.

I wasn't the only one who slept on the flight, so we're all a little bleary-eyed as we check into our rooms, which are conveniently located in the same stretch of hallway in a ritzy hotel.

Last time I stayed somewhere on assignment, it was a tiny little brick motel somewhere between Buffalo and Rochester, and I only stopped because my rental car got a flat tire on the long drive back to the city.

So, suffice it to say, this is a major upgrade.

After my post-flight face-washing and thorough teeth-brushing, I'm feeling like a new human as we regroup and head to rehearsal.

When we arrive, Dan and I are given lanyards

announcing us as "CREW," then Leigh ushers us down the aisle of the venue.

It's a little eerie to see such a large space so empty.

"This gives you a pass to go wherever you want," she explains. "Dan, you might want to sync up with the sound crew here. They usually know the best angles for capturing footage, and they've already been given a rundown of the show, where the lighting kicks and what the breaks are and so on."

"On it," he says, picking up his camera and gear before heading toward the sound booth in the back.

"So, what do you usually do during rehearsal?" I ask Leigh.

"There's always some emergency that I need to oversee, whether it's replacing or repairing damaged equipment, resolving costume issues, or addressing the fact we don't have enough press passes."

I quirk an eyebrow. "And you do that as a *publicist?*"

"Well, heaven forbid Devin actually do his job," she retorts, then abruptly blinks as if suddenly remembering who she's talking to. "Please don't tell anyone. Or put that in the documentary somehow."

I laugh. "I don't think the *Exos* audience cares about your opinion on Devin. No offense."

"None taken," she says with a smile. "How about I show you around?"

"That would be great."

She leads me through the back, and even though the theater is nearly empty, a beefy-looking security guy pointedly eyes our badges before nodding in confirmation and letting us pass.

"This is the green room," Leigh says, pointing to a small room just off the stage.

Inside, monitors display the soundcheck that's just getting started on the stage.

I watch for a little too long as Travis fiddles around on his beautiful matte black guitar, then I take in the assortment of drinks and snacks set up in the room itself.

"Why is there a bowl of green Skittles?" I ask curiously.

"Oh," she laughs. "It's in the tour rider, among a list of other specifics like equipment and tuning and things they'll need. Phoenix is really particular about his drum kit and made a huge fuss about it during their first tour together. And Travis heard that Van Halen used to specify in theirs that they wanted a bowl of M&M's with all the brown ones removed. They, apparently, used the request to get a sense of how thorough the venues were when addressing a band's criteria."

"Interesting. Has it proven to be effective?"

She nods. "Only a handful of places have messed it up over the years. But, honestly, I don't think it makes a real difference other than giving Phoenix an excuse to eat a massive handful of candy before he runs on stage."

I chuckle. "Well, I can't blame him for that. If I had to perform in front of that many people, I'd need to be hopped up on sugar, too."

"No, same," she says. "You'd think I'd be fine with being in front of the public, given my profession, but one time, Travis asked me to introduce him at an award cere-mony, and I almost fainted."

My eyes widen when we enter a surprisingly large space

that serves as the band's dressing room. I assumed that the guys wore their own clothes for performances.

But there is an entire rack of clothes set aside for Nick, and another for Phoenix, while Travis has *two* of them to himself, consisting of shirts, floral patterned vests, sleek blazers, and at least a dozen pairs of ripped jeans.

"Do they wear something new every night?" I ask, running my fingertips along some faded denim.

"Oh, yes, they have to," Leigh explains. "Not only because of the aesthetic but because of how hard they go on stage."

"What do you mean?" I question.

"It's like a workout and frat party all at once. They are constantly on the move for their ninety-minute set, and that's *after* their adrenaline-fueled warm-up session in here—"

"So they're just letting anyone back here, then?" Devin interrupts as he saunters in, still wearing his sunglasses despite the fact we're inside.

Leigh offers him a pinched smile. "Apparently."

"Anything for me to take care of right now?" he asks. "No grand emergencies or people to schmooze?"

"Other than Dakota, no."

I snort. "I'm hardly in need of schmoozing."

"Good," Devin says mid-yawn. "I'll be napping in the green room if you need me."

Leigh's eyes narrow at his retreat.

"Nice guy," I say under my breath. "So, what else is there to see around here?"

She shakes off her agitation as she gives me her attention again. "Aside from a loading dock, not much else. I need to grab some pictures for social media, so if you want to join me and watch the process for yourself, you're totally welcome to. Unless you want to wander for a bit?"

"Watching sounds good," I tell her.

And that's what I do for the rest of the night.

The band spends more than an hour running through their set and making adjustments based on what they weren't happy with the night before.

The intro to their third song, "The Night," was apparently too rushed for Travis's taste, so they run through it three times the proper way. After that, as they're running through the rest of the list, Nick suggests switching up the second song of the encore.

Personally, I think it's annoying that bands do a whole fake leaving thing before they come back on.

But Leigh explains it gives them time to down water and catch their breath before finishing out the night on a high note, and while I see her point, I still think it's strange.

After everything is ready, we all gather backstage for dinner in the green room.

It feels more like a family gathering than work. Nearly two dozen crew members join the musicians, and everyone involved in the production stuffs their faces and chatters happily.

Well, with a couple of exceptions.

I grab a sandwich and observe from a corner while Dan runs back into the empty auditorium to change the batteries in the camera that's going to take a time lapse of the theater filling up.

When the meal is done and the doors of the venue have

officially opened, I peek from behind the curtain to watch excited fans run in and try to get as close to the stage as possible. I note at least three hand-painted signs and several shirts from previous tours before I head back to the dressing room.

"Hey," Travis says as I enter.

"Hey," I return, taking a seat where he had been fiddling with his hair earlier. "You ready?"

He nods and double-checks his pockets for guitar picks.

"Does this shade of foundation make me look too orange?" Phoenix asks as he scrutinizes his cheekbones in the lighted mirror.

"No," Nick says coolly as he leans against the counter beside me. "Personally, I love the Oompa Loompa vibe."

Phoenix rolls his eyes and looks to Travis for his opinion, who shrugs before answering.

"I mean, dude, you are wearing a green shirt..."

"Both of you are useless," Phoenix mutters, stepping away from the mirror and grabbing a beer from the table.

I stifle my snicker as the door opens.

"Welcome backstage, ladies," Devin announces, waving in a group of teenage girls.

My stomach clenches at the sight because it's too familiar to the scenario from the music video shoot.

"They won a pre-show meet and greet with Travis," Nick quickly explains.

"Oh," I breathe out in relief.

We both flinch at the winners' high-pitched screams of excitement, then watch in amusement as Travis very patiently poses for photos and signs their shirts.

They pepper him with questions for nearly a half hour

straight until the opening act starts up, then Devin proves useful enough to escort them back to their seats in the audience.

After they're gone, I join the band in the green room to watch the performance. But even after Dan and Leigh join us, there's no small talk because when the music starts, Travis, Phoenix, and Nick are absorbed by it.

I guess I expect them to sit back and enjoy it while still laughing and talking, but instead, it's like it signals that they're going to be on soon, so they use the time to mentally prepare.

Phoenix taps his pointer fingers to the beat against his kneecaps, while Nick closes his eyes and takes intentional deep breaths.

But, of course, it's Travis who steals my attention with his look of intensity as he watches the lead singer move around the stage and scream into the microphone.

His enthrallment makes me nervous, like he's a predator scoping out what he's soon to attack and devour.

And I find it absurdly alluring.

"All right, boys," Devin says, stomping into the room and jarring us all from our quiet thoughts and reflections. "Warm-up's done. Let's get this shit going."

The three of them stand up as if taking a cue, like this is the signal they've been waiting for.

They huddle in the center of the room, arms across one another's shoulders as they whisper, swaying side to side as the roar of the crowd increases.

Dan quirks an eyebrow at me before he picks up the camera and starts filming.

"They do this before every show," Leigh explains. "It's tradition."

Wordlessly, I nod.

"Let's do this shit!" Devin finally yells.

The trio breaks off in smiles and happy whoops.

Phoenix reaches for a handful of Skittles before they all file out toward the stage.

I can't help but try the candy for myself as excited screams fill my ears and the first strum of a guitar kicks off the concert.

TWELVE

I'm *really* trying to maintain some journalistic integrity while on this assignment, but when Leigh brings me a celebratory beer as Travis belts out the vocals to the final song of the night, it's hard not to indulge.

The post-show high is contagious, with endorphins running wild as the guys all practically skip off the stage with smiles on their faces. That only increases when they immediately start pounding tequila shots in the dressing room.

Dan is glued to his camera, as he has been all night, and I know the footage he's getting is pure gold.

"Great show," I congratulate Nick.

He beams at me over a very full mixed drink. "Thanks. I was a little off on 'Imposter Syndrome,' though. I'm sure Travis is going to ream me for it during rehearsal tomorrow."

I laugh and catch Dan's eye over Nick's shoulder, knowing that this is getting recorded.

"Is he a hard-ass when it comes to that kind of stuff?" I ask.

"A hard-ass?" Nick says lightly. "I had drill sergeants in military school who were more lenient than him."

I take a sip of my drink as my brows rise in surprise. "You went to military school?"

"Before I dropped out of high school, yeah." He smirks. "It was a last-ditch effort by my parents to, uh, *straighten* me out."

"That's awful," I say with a frown.

"Well, that's what—" Nick stops abruptly, growling at something behind me.

I turn to see Devin leading a crowd of women into the room, and I'm relieved they all look to be of age.

But the dressing room already felt like it was at capacity, and now it's stuffed. I'm forced to take another step toward Nick, and though his entire demeanor deflates, I know I'm not the cause.

"Oh, no," Leigh sighs in disapproval as she appears at my side.

The three of us watch as the women, encouraged by Devin, sidle up to the crew and help themselves to the plethora of alcohol.

When Phoenix gestures to a redhead to join him on the armchair, Nick mumbles an excuse and leaves the room.

"I'd better try to do some damage control," Leigh mutters, glaring at Phoenix as he laughs heartily at something a crew member said to him.

"Okay," I say sympathetically.

As she shoves her way through to follow Nick, I try to

make my way over to Dan, who has become my safety net every time I'm at a loss for what to do with myself.

But before I get there, Devin steps into my path. "Journalist," he says.

"Brother *slash* manager," I return.

"Enjoying the party?"

"I am, thank you."

"Aren't you going to ask me any questions?" he demands, beckoning Dan over with one hand while locking the other around the waist of a giggling fan.

"Would love to," I say flatly.

Devin winks at me. "Go ahead. I'm an open book."

"Can you tell me a little bit about what's happening right now? Narrate it for the audience?"

"We're living our lives to the fullest," he says jovially. "Celebrating a successful show on the West Coast, and since we don't have to travel tonight, we can go extra hard."

Devin squeezes the side of his companion, which sets off another round of high-pitched laughter.

I swallow my impulse to gag. "How many tours have you been on with Travis?"

"I've lost count. But I've been with him since the beginning. Number one fan and all that."

"You didn't officially become his manager until he signed with the mainstream label," I remind him, recalling my research. "Isn't that right?"

"Technically, yeah," he says with a shrug.

"And what were you doing before that?"

"I was an entrepreneur. Worked with a few businesses, but when Travis needed someone, I couldn't say no. Since then, it's been a hell of a ride, watching him succeed and supporting him. I'm probably the proudest big brother on the planet."

"Touching," I reply dryly. "When you were kids, did you have any indication that Travis would be a big star?"

"Yeah," Devin says confidently. "I was the one who told him to really go for it, you know? It was actually *my* guitar that he started playing on back then."

"Did he know even then this was what he wanted to do?"

"You'll have to ask him," Devin says after downing the dregs of his drink. "But I think that's enough interviewing for right now. There's alcohol to be consumed."

I purse my lips. "Right."

He retreats into the crowd, calling for a round of cheers.

"Was any of that usable?" I ask my coconspirator.

"Hard to tell," Dan shrugs. "We can take a look at the footage tomorrow."

"Sounds like a plan." I pick at the label of my beer. "Well, if you think you've got this, I think I'm going to head out. I doubt we'll get any other good soundbites tonight."

Dan smiles as one of the crew members opens a bottle of champagne. "I'll stick around for a little longer for some B-roll."

"I'll text you in the morning, then?"

"Yeah," he says with a nod.

It takes me a few minutes to get through the crowd, and just as I'm about to step through the exit, I realize my purse is missing.

In a slight panic, considering the size of the venue and

the number of people in it, I quickly run through the last few hours and recall I last had it in the green room.

I double back and breathe a sigh of relief when my eyes land on it, sitting innocently next to the couch I occupied earlier.

"Hey," Travis says.

I jolt at the sound of his voice. "What are you doing in here?"

He gestures around with his beer bottle. "Decompressing."

"Alone? In the dark?"

"I just needed a minute," he admits.

"Okay," I relent in understanding. "I'll leave you to it, then."

"Dakota." He says my name like a plea, and that slight vulnerability halts me in my tracks. "Join me, will you?"

I turn and see the same challenging look he gave me at the club on the night of his shoe release, only this time, there's no venom in his eyes.

He holds out a fresh beer for me.

I tell myself that I accept it and join him because our relationship is still fragile, and I need to do everything I can to bridge the gap between us.

But as I take that first sip, I appreciate how the low lighting of the hallway casts shadows and highlights on his features, increasing the severity of his angles.

"So, what'd you think?" Travis asks.

"Of what?"

"The show."

I take a sip of my beer. "Honestly?"

He nods. "Honestly."

"Fucking incredible," I say with a sigh.

Travis smirks. "Well, don't sound so upset about it."

"I am supposed to remain as neutral as I can," I remind him.

"You're still allowed to enjoy the experience."

"Funny, that's what my editor said. Well, a slightly different version of that."

He nods. "I understand I'm different than the usual subjects of your reporting."

"That's an understatement." I take a long pull of beer. "I'm just glad I insisted on experiencing the show in the audience before this because I think you've ruined concerts for me forever."

"I'll take that as a compliment."

"You should," I say, tucking a lock of hair behind my ear. "So, how do you think it went?"

He rests his head back against the cushion before he answers. "I think I want to switch back to the setlist we used in New York, but overall, things flowed as I wanted them to. I need to work on my intro for the chorus of 'Vantage Point,' and Nick was a little slow on 'Imposter Syndrome.'"

I laugh. "He said you'd say that."

"And they say musicians are unpredictable and wild," he drawls.

I smile. "So, this is what you do after a show? Decompress and think through every little mistake?"

"Well, usually we're off to the hotel to sleep it off and get ready to travel the next day. It's not the norm for us to play the same city right away, but it worked out with scheduling and demand."

"Got it."

"But yeah. I like to run through everything when it's fresh."

"Dude, don't fucking say this shit to me!" Nick snaps in the hallway.

I sit up and blink, surprised to hear such forcefulness coming from someone I've considered sweet and quiet.

"Come on," Phoenix shoots back. "You always get like this. It's nothing."

Nick laughs, loud and hollow. "Nothing? *Nothing?* You were practically feeling that girl up."

Travis sighs before he stands up and crosses the room.

I expect him to tell them off or jump in somehow, but he merely closes the door slowly, ensuring they're not disturbed by the sound, before he slumps back into his chair.

"They'll be fucking as soon as they're done fighting," he tells me, tone a little snippy.

"Another part of the post-show ritual?" I ask lightly.

Travis bites his bottom lip. "Something like that."

"I was talking to your brother earlier," I admit, pivoting the conversation back to him. "He said you picked up a guitar when you were young. Is this what you always wanted to do?"

"I don't see any cameras around," Travis says coolly.

"This is me asking you," I press. "I don't remember you being particularly musically inclined in high school. When you bothered to show up, that is."

Travis drops his now empty bottle on the table and cracks open another one. "I don't have some magical story where I picked up a guitar and knew this was what I wanted. It was just kind of there. I'd get high and play because I needed something to do with my hands. And that's pretty much what high school was like for me. One joint after another. Then the next thing I knew, we were graduating, and my mom needed help with rent."

His eyes lock on mine.

"So when the girl I shared the shift with at the taco place, and occasionally fucked in my car, told me she was pregnant and that it was mine, I kind of lost it and threw myself into my music."

"But you don't have…" I trail off.

"It came out months later that she faked the whole thing. She was hoping that by being together, it would actually happen."

"And it took years for you to get divorced?"

He tilts his head at me. "You know about that?"

"Public record," I admit, feeling a little ashamed.

If he regrets opening up to me, he doesn't show it. "We went through some shit, then I went through some shit, and now I'm going through other shit."

"But being a rich and famous musician seemed like the easiest path for you to take with your life?" I tease, trying to lighten the mood.

Travis snorts. "Actually, the first job I got in the industry paid me twelve bucks an hour. Bouncer at a club."

I skeptically eye his frame because although he's tall, he's lean and not exactly what I would categorize as the normal build for that job.

"Don't size me up," he scolds playfully before taking another sip. "Man, I was so stoked when I got that first paycheck. I'm pretty sure I still have it at home somewhere."

"It's always good to remember where you came from."

He rubs the back of his neck. "Yeah."

A silence settles over us, and although it's comfortable, I want to know more.

"And then what happened?" I ask. "After the very lucrative bouncer gig?"

"There was an open mic night on Tuesdays. Took me almost a year to gather up the courage to play my guitar and sing some of the random shit I'd written down. But I did it. Then I got more confident, started posting on YouTube, and eventually, the club owners started paying me to perform. Things kind of spiraled from there."

I consider that explanation for a moment. "You know, back when you still gave interviews, everyone hailed you as some big, overnight success."

"That's the weird thing about all this. People just see me as some kid who skyrocketed to the top, but I can't tell you how many times I had to drive across town on a nearly empty tank of gas just to play a fifteen-minute set to a practically non-existent audience."

"Well, that certainly makes sense, given the story you told in your music video," I say.

Travis shifts and turns his body toward me. "What about you? Is being a successful reporter everything you hoped it would be?"

"Yes and no. I was so single-minded about writing and interviewing and researching for a living that it kind of became my entire life." I pause, surprised at how freely I can admit this to Travis when I haven't even realized it in my own head yet. "This is the first time in years I've done anything out of my routine."

"And? Is it a good or a bad thing?"

"Good. I think. I mean, I've been going and going since high school, so I don't think I ever stopped to really think about that."

"I know," Travis admits. "I remember. So driven and determined, even then."

I look down at the beer in my hands as my cheeks flush.

"That's strange to think about, honestly," I say, bringing my eyes back up to his. "The teenage version of myself that's rooted in your memories."

He blinks at my word choice.

I blame my vulnerability on the alcohol, so I stand and toss the empty bottle in the recycling bin. "I should probably get going."

"Okay," Travis says.

"Okay," I return.

When I turn around for one final look at him as I open the door, I catch him scribbling away in his little black notebook.

THIRTEEN

The next few days—and cities—blur together.

It's all so new to Dan and me that we approach every venue and experience with fresh eyes and interest, but I start to sympathize with how months and years of this can compound into burnout.

And this is just one piece of it all, really.

Because the recording time, marketing and press engagements, and touring, all while trying to maintain their dysfunctional personal lives, seem pretty intense.

Despite Travis's reassurance that the pair would patch things up, Nick and Phoenix are awkward around each other for the second performance in Los Angeles, then the ones following in Las Vegas, Reno, and Boise.

By the time we sit down to do an interview with Phoenix and Nick in San Francisco, they're so irritated with each other that the tension has bubbled up to impact everyone else, even Dan and me.

"Tell me about your first performance together," I prompt. "What was it like?"

"Fine," Nick says.

"Yeah," Phoenix breathes, jaw clenched.

"What city was it in?" I ask, desperate to try and get anything usable. "How did it go?"

It's the thirteenth time I've tried to engage them, and once again, I'm met with crossed arms and one-word answers.

I look to Dan to see if he has any ideas, but he merely frowns and shakes his head.

"Maybe we should try this another day," I finally suggest.

"Sounds good," Nick says, jumping up in relief, though he offers me an apologetic shrug before he leaves.

Phoenix bolts from the room without a word.

"Great," Dan says flippantly.

I tug at the ends of my hair. "Definitely not ideal."

"Ideal? This is a fucking disaster."

I quirk a brow at his frustration. "Where is this coming from?"

He sits down beside me and sighs. "Look, the footage isn't great, and our story is barely held together with anecdotal scenes. This isn't just a long piece where you can clarify quotes over a phone call later. We need *interviews* with actual *people*."

"I don't appreciate your condescension, Dan," I tell him evenly. "I'm well aware of how to tell a story."

"Well, I don't see why you keep having all these conversations with Travis Young without recording them! We're here to work, not make friends."

"You don't seem to have a problem with that when you're getting wined and dined," I retort, and before he can open his mouth, I hold up a finger, signaling to let me finish. "But back to the issue at hand. Yes. We need interviews."

"We need interviews," he agrees.

"I know the perfect person," I say, leaving him behind momentarily as I walk away with purpose.

I cross the expansive lobby and the entrance into the swanky hotel bar and restaurant.

Even on the road, I'm starting to notice some routines surfacing, so I'm not surprised to find Leigh on a barstool, stirring a specialty cocktail.

"You're coming with me," I order her, dropping a twenty to cover the cost of her drink.

"What's wrong?" Leigh asks. "I thought you'd be happy."

"Happy?" I balk. "Phoenix and Nick just walked out of yet another interview. We have nothing to go off of at this point, Leigh."

"I just..." She blinks. "Never mind. Well, I can talk to them and see if they're willing to sit separately or something."

I tug on her wrist and practically drag her to the conference room. "That would be great. But for now, you're going to be on camera."

"What?" she demands as Dan smiles at her arrival. "No way."

"Yes way," I say adamantly.

"But, Dakota, I'm a behind-the-scenes publicity person.

135

In the background. You know I don't like to do this sort of thing."

I shake my head, dismissing her excuses. "You know Travis Young better than most people at this point, and we need interviews."

"Can I at least go change?" Leigh whines.

I glance at her dress, noting the bottom is slightly wrinkled from traveling. "We'll frame it from the waist up."

"You really must be desperate," she says.

Dan gestures for her to sit on the stool.

"Yep," I say, handing over the clip-on microphone.

"Ugh, fine," she grumbles.

Once Dan runs her through a quick soundcheck and takes his position behind the monitor, I sit down to the right of the setup, intentionally angling us so she's talking to me and not staring directly down the lens, which I know can be intimidating.

"Just a reminder," Dan says in a pleasant voice. "We're only going to use the best parts of your interview for soundbites, so no pressure on you at all. Even though you're the *only* sit-down we have at the moment."

"Dan," I warn him.

"Sorry." He drops his gaze and focuses on working the equipment. "But it's important that you ignore the camera as best you can and just talk to Dakota like you normally would. Well, minus the microphone and lighting and everything."

"Okay," Leigh breathes.

"Tell me your name and your association with Travis," I begin.

"I'm Leigh Baker, and I'm Travis's publicist. I do a

number of things for him, but mostly I keep his name out of the press as much as possible."

"And as I understand it, you *actually* have been a part of managing and progressing Travis's career forward, unlike Devin."

She laughs, and I watch the tension dissipate slightly as her posture softens. "No comment on that one."

"Fair enough." I return her smile. "I was hoping we could start at the beginning, anyway. Let's go back to your first meeting with Travis. What was that like?"

"I have a pretty interesting story of how I got this job," she admits, wringing her hands.

"Really?" I shift and settle deeper into my chair, getting comfortable. "What happened?"

"Well, I was an intern on the marketing team when he signed, and I was mostly stuck getting coffee and taking notes, those kinds of things. About three weeks in, I somehow got put in charge of coordinating schedules and meetings, and as luck and inexperience would have it, I double-booked my boss for a meeting with Travis and another artist."

"Oh, no," I groan.

She nods. "I was so mortified, and my boss was pissed. I was surprised he didn't outright fire me, but as some sort of weird punishment, which obviously didn't turn out to be the hardship he hoped, he tasked me with entertaining Travis for two hours until he would be free himself."

"Entertain?" I clarify.

"From what I knew about Travis and his reputation, I assumed he'd be annoyed at wasting time just sitting around. But we hung out in one of the conference rooms, ordered in lunch on the company dime, listened to music, and took turns flicking paper footballs across the table."

She stops and smiles at the memory.

"In that time, I confessed that I had supremely fucked up and conveyed how desperate I was for the cash and the job. I was so deeply embarrassed."

"And how did Travis react?"

Leigh's eyes lock onto mine as she straightens up to deliver her next line. "When my boss came in making apologies to Travis and throwing me under the bus, Travis told him that he only wanted to work with me moving forward, which essentially guaranteed my employment at the label."

"Really?"

She nods. "Eventually, I quit and became his full-time publicist instead of remaining in my position as marketing liaison. But I can't even begin to think where I'd be if he hadn't said something."

"Wow," I say. "That was a very selfless thing for him to do for a total stranger."

She pauses and takes a breath. "That's the thing about Travis. He has this big reputation as a bad boy, but really, he'd do anything for anyone who needed it. Have you heard about the charity he started in Pittsburgh?"

I turn to Dan, who gives me a thumbs-up, and it feels like a weight has been lifted off my shoulders.

Finally, someone is opening up and diving deeper into who Travis Young really is.

For the next hour, Leigh tells me about the work Travis has done to fund music programs for kids in the town where we grew up—all of which has been done anonymously.

We also learn about the single mother who worked on his crew for his first tour, and when he got his first big payday, he bought her a modest house outside of New Orleans for her entire family.

I eat up every single word and story, eager for more about who he is.

But when Leigh really hits her stride, I sense that she's sidestepping details, intentionally leaving out anecdotes about past girlfriends and run-ins with the law, but we get enough material that I feel far less pressure than I did before I kidnapped her from the bar.

"Thanks again for doing this," I tell her after we wrap.

"It wasn't as terrible as I thought it would be," she admits as she hands Dan the microphone.

"That's what she said," he quips.

I roll my eyes as Leigh laughs.

My phone rings, and I pull it out of my pocket to see it's Mark, which is both unexpected and nerve-wracking. I hope he doesn't have more bad news about Travis.

"Sorry," I say to them. "I should take this."

"Go ahead," Leigh says, a sparkle in her eye.

I nod and step out before I answer. "Hello?"

"Dakota," Mark greets me with joy. "You'll never guess where I am."

"You know I hate when people make me play guessing games," I say with a frown. "Just tell me."

"Don't look so sad, Dakota Shaw."

I stop in my tracks and glance around until my eyes

land on him and the weekend bag slung around his shoulders.

"Surprise!" he says before rushing over and pulling me into a hug.

I back out of his embrace. "What are you doing here?" I ask flatly.

"I wanted to see you."

I blink rapidly, having no response for that.

"Have fun," Leigh singsongs as she passes, walking over to the bar with Dan.

As I watch her go, I lock eyes with Travis, who's chewing on ice cubes rather aggressively and tilting his head, apparently trying to suss out what the hell is happening.

I wish I had an answer for that myself.

FOURTEEN

Rarely in my life am I shocked into silence, but this is one of those times.

Mark chats happily as I lead him up to my hotel room, one that I planned to enjoy later, *alone*, with a long, post-show soak in the oversized tub.

"...and then she actually fell asleep on me! Snoring and everything. The flight attendant couldn't stop laughing."

"Mark," I cut him off as the door closes behind us. "What in the actual fuck are you doing here?"

He balks. "What do you mean? I'm here to see you, like I said."

"But why?" I press.

Maybe I'm being a little direct and cold, but I'm floored by the turn of events.

"I hadn't heard from you in a while—"

"It's barely been three weeks," I argue. "We normally don't talk for months at a time."

He swallows. "I saw you in that music video."

"Something I still haven't brought myself to watch," I mumble.

"And after reading thousands of speculative comments and seeing some of the recent paparazzi pictures, I had to come see for myself."

"See *what* exactly?" I demand.

"If you and Travis Young are together."

I burst out laughing. "What the hell are you talking about?"

"The way you looked at each other in the video and how you basically gave up your whole career to go on tour with him. It just didn't make any sense. Or at least, I didn't want it to. So I impulse-bought a ticket."

"Mark," I sigh.

"And then on the plane ride here," he continues. "I realized how batshit-crazy that was, but since I was already in the air and already had the time off work, I figured I would make a nice little trip of it and tag along with you."

"Mark," I repeat slowly.

He smiles brightly at me. "Dakota."

"This is insane. Like, absolutely insane. You cannot use my *work* as a vacation."

"It's just a few nights."

"Just a few nights?" I sputter.

He shrugs. "It'll be fun. And besides, you owe me, remember?"

I grind my molars before I respond, somewhat baffled by his audacity. "Owing you is buying dinner next time I'm visiting my parents, not giving you a warm welcome when you invite yourself to my hotel room across the country."

Finally, Mark looks sheepish. "Shit, you're really mad about this, aren't you?"

"What gave you that idea?" I snap.

He sighs. "Your boss seemed to think it was a nice gesture."

My hands are shaking in anger. "You talked to Bryan?"

"Well, we've kind of kept in touch after that company holiday party you took me to—"

"*Four years ago?*" I shriek and pull at the ends of my hair.

Mark backs away slowly as I try to compose myself.

It's hard to believe that, years ago, I saw a future with Mark. I thought we were on the same page, enjoying each other's presence and making our relationship work long-distance, under the assumption that someday we'd figure it out.

But when it became clear that I wasn't going to leave New York and all Mark's contacts were in Pittsburgh, we just kind of gradually ended things—only to pick them back up again when I'd go back and visit.

And it has never been clearer that things *really* need to be over between us until right now.

"I'm an idiot," Mark says. "A total fucking idiot."

"You are," I confirm.

"This was a ridiculous idea."

"I agree."

"But we should have sex."

I narrow my gaze at him. "You're joking."

"Kind of," he says lightly. "I was just hoping you'd continue to back up everything I said."

Despite how irritated I am with him, that brings a very small smile to my face. "Mark."

"I fucked up royally. I'll see if the hotel can grab me another room on the way out."

"The way out?" I drawl.

"Well, Bryan said that Leigh left a badge for me at the front desk..."

"After all this, you think you still get a backstage pass to see Travis perform?" I ask.

"Well, yeah," Mark answers without question. "I did fly all the way out here."

"Because you were worried about circumstances that impact *your* goals for us," I interject. "Not mine."

He blinks and takes a step back like I've slapped him.

"Mark, we should have cut this off a long time ago," I admit. "Ever since we ended our relationship officially and then, well, continued things, I think things have gotten complicated."

"You're right," he says a little dejectedly. "So, it's really over, then?"

"Yes," I say resolutely.

"Okay."

And he looks so sad and depressed in that moment that it guts me.

I sigh. "So if you tag along, it's *just* as friends...who are going to need a very defined break for the next few months. Or years. Decades, maybe."

His sadness disappears almost instantly. "Does that mean I can come?"

I nod. "We should get going."

"Yeah?" he says brightly.

"We don't want to miss soundcheck," I tell him.

His grin is so wide, it nearly splits his face in half. "Absolutely not."

Mark follows me as we walk to the venue, which is only a few blocks from our hotel.

I'm able to give him a tour without even getting one for myself—I get the basic gist by now; we typically have a separate dressing room and green room at each venue—and he indulges in a handful of green Skittles as the band plays.

As Mark *oohs* and *aahs* at every little thing, I'm tempted to strangle him, but it is a good reminder of the once in a lifetime experience I am getting.

And that it's already almost half over.

We're only scheduled to follow Travis Young along this leg of his tour, and that thought is a reminder that Dan and I still have *so* much work to do.

It doesn't help matters that my ex-boyfriend showed up.

Which is why, after soundcheck, I send Mark back to the hotel until showtime so Dan and I can get some work done.

We camp out in the corner of the dressing room, running through Leigh's interview twice to pick out the most impactful quotes.

We're at a good stopping point when the band comes in to get changed, but I keep my eyes glued to the screen, no matter how much I want to stare at Travis's tattoo-covered abs.

When the guys are dressed, I finally pull myself away from the monitor and stretch.

Devin leads the band through their pre-show ritual, and although Nick and Phoenix can't even look at each other, they all break out into smiles before they take the stage.

"Dakota?" Mark calls from the doorway. "Am I late?"

"No, you're fine, come on in," I say, waving him over. "Dan, this is Mark. Mark, Dan."

They shake hands and extend pleasantries.

"Well, we should probably get to it," I exhale and stand up.

"Who's this?" Devin says curiously, wandering back into the dressing room.

I sigh. "Mark, Devin. Devin, Mark."

"Nice to meet you," Mark says, keeping his cool even though they both size each other up.

"You too," Devin returns. "Beer?"

"Oh, no," I start. "We—"

"Would love to," Mark inserts, smiling as Devin pops the top off a bottle for him. "So, you work with Travis?"

Devin snorts. "I'm practically part of the band," he boasts. "I'm Travis's manager. And brother."

"Touring is pretty normal for you, then?"

I don't know what Mark is playing at, but I merely stand there, slightly gobsmacked as they bro out, chatting and drinking together.

"Shit," Devin says suddenly as he checks his phone. "Leigh says there's an issue with the soundboard. I have to run, but I'll catch you after."

"Sounds good," Mark calls after him.

I roll my eyes as my ex smiles at me. "Come on," I mutter. "Let's go watch the show."

He follows me as I lead the way to the wings.

"Do you want to tell me what the hell you're up to?" I ask as he settles in beside me, gaze fixed on the stage.

146

Mark shrugs. "I'm going to make this whole disaster up to you somehow."

I give him some serious side-eye. "Please don't."

"Something's off about that guy Devin," he insists, leaning in to be heard over the loud music.

"You got that from three seconds of conversation?" I ask.

"I just got a weird vibe from him. Call it private detective instincts, but I'm going to figure out what it is, and you can do whatever you want with that information."

"I thought you were here as my friend, not on the job?"

"Who says I can't do both?" he poses.

The lights of the stage go dark in rhythm with the drum solo that Phoenix is absolutely crushing, and Mark gets distracted momentarily by the showmanship of it all.

I roll my eyes at his visceral delight. "Well, at least we're flying out tomorrow to our next city and show. And you are not included in the 'we' of that sentence, Mark."

He laughs and puts an arm around my shoulders. "If there's one thing I can tell you for certain, Dakota, it's that I'm never going to assume I'm a part of a 'we' with you ever again."

"Good," I say, smiling up at him.

"But this is fucking awesome," he breathes.

While Mark tries to take it all in—the musicians, the audience, the projections on the screen behind them—I only have eyes for Travis.

There's something magical about watching him on stage, like I'm watching art get created as he moves his body, and I let myself get caught up in the performance to drown out everything else.

FIFTEEN

Somewhere between songs in the encore set, Devin and Mark crack open beers in the green room. Once the final clang on the drum hits and the lights fall, Devin chugs the remainder of his beer.

"We're all going out to a club," he announces, standing proudly in the middle of the room. "No excuses!"

Leigh seems exasperated by the entire situation. "Our flight is at ten o'clock tomorrow morning."

"I've already scheduled the wake-up call," he assures her. "Who's with me?"

"Hard pass," Leigh says.

"I'm totally in, dude." Mark stands up to do that odd handshake-then-hug thing.

"Same," Dan says.

"Only if the camera stays behind," Devin insists. "Debauchery is not a part of this documentary."

"Fine," Dan agrees.

"I'm with Leigh," I say, clearly surprising her.

She smiles and loops her arm through mine. "Come on, let's go get some cocktails at the hotel bar."

"See you later, Dakota," Mark calls with a wink.

Leigh and I make our way outside and walk along the crowded sidewalks, exchanging small talk until we return to the hotel.

"Why aren't you going out with Mark?" Leigh asks once we've placed our drink orders.

I sigh back against the cushy material of the booth. "His coming here was a mistake."

She winces. "I'm so sorry. Bryan made it seem like it was a good thing, but I should have guessed you're the type of person who doesn't like surprises."

"Yes," I say. "But it's fine. Gave us the opportunity to clear the air and officially move on."

"Well, good."

The server returns with our beverages, dropping them in front of us before scurrying off back to the bar again.

"How'd the footage from earlier turn out?" Leigh asks, thankfully not prolonging the conversation about Mark or anything related to my personal life.

"Great actually," I say. "Thanks again for doing that."

"Well, it's not like I volunteered, but I am happy you guys got something you can use."

I chuckle. "Hopefully the first of many good interviews."

"Cheers to that," Leigh says, clinking the rim of my drink with hers.

"Cheers," I return before taking a sip. "Wow, this is good."

"I'm somewhat of a cocktail connoisseur," she jokes.

"Did you take a mixology class or something?"

She shakes her head. "I just spend a lot of time alone at bars around the world."

That makes both of us laugh.

"You don't go out with the guys?" I ask.

"I did at first, especially back when Travis was in his partying days. I think we were all just so excited to have people paying for our meals, and the freedom to do whatever the hell we wanted, that we went a little wild with it." She pauses and smiles at me over the rim of her glass. "But I'm sure it's nothing you didn't experience at those early *Exos* parties."

"Absolutely not," I say with a snort. "From the time we've spent together, can you really imagine *me* partaking in any of that?"

Leigh runs her gaze over my hair, which, despite today's emotional turmoil, is just as pin-straight as always, then takes in my starched, wrinkle-free button-down that's tucked into my high-waist pants.

It's not that people who are held together as intentionally and rigidly as I am don't have wild streaks—it's just that I'm not the type of person to really let go, and it's fairly obvious.

Especially when compared to the people I've been surrounded with on this tour.

"I guess not," she says, scrunching her nose. "I'm just going off the word of one of my publicity friends. She admitted she gave some guy a blowjob in the women's bathroom at an *Exos* holiday party."

I snort. "That sounds about right. Working in a newsroom, especially in Brooklyn, is like another iteration of college."

"But you don't participate?"

"Not really."

"Well, I guess that's how you had your first story submitted for a Pulitzer before you turned twenty-five," she says lightly.

"And look at me now," I tease before taking a long sip of my drink.

Leigh chuckles. "I'm sure all this is strange for you."

"Mostly just how normal this is for you," I admit. "Private jets, screaming fans, endless drinks, photo shoots, paparazzi...all of it."

"I'm just trying to enjoy the perks while I can," she tells me.

I quirk a brow at her. "That sounds ominous."

"It's reality, I think. It's ridiculous to say this because I'm only thirty years old, but how much longer can I be expected to run around chasing musicians and doing Devin's job for him?"

She takes a sizable sip of alcohol, giving herself a minute to stop the rant before it starts.

I watch her with a bit of dread.

As much as I appreciate the way the blueberry and elderflower flavors mask the vodka, I'm already feeling buzzed after one drink.

The server, though, magically reappears with another round for us before I've even thought to ask for one.

"It's just funny," she says, trading her empty glass for the fresh drink.

"What is?" I ask as we silently cheers.

"Life."

I nod. "Yes."

"From the outside looking in, I'm sure being on tour and in the studio seems so great," she says quietly, glass hovering near her face. "But in reality, it's just not what everyone expects or dreams up. I've learned that from Travis."

The words settle between us, and I break the momentary silence with an audible sigh.

She hiccups. "Excuse me," she says quickly, blushing and pushing her half-full drink away. "I guess that's my cue to head to bed."

"Thanks for the cocktails, Leigh. And the company."

"Anytime." She grins and pats my hand once, then she heads off.

I take another sip, then pull out my phone, wondering if I should text Mark to see what he's up to.

But ultimately, I decide against it because, frankly, I really don't fucking feel like it.

Instead, I simply sit and take a minute for myself.

Has it really only been a few weeks since I sat in Bryan's office and got my entire life and routine derailed by this assignment?

For some reason, it feels like much longer than that, or maybe I'm just getting used to this temporary life of everything I'll never experience again.

"Where's your boyfriend?" Travis asks, looming over the table with his hands shoved in his pockets.

"Nonexistent," I retort, covering my shock at his sudden appearance.

He quirks an eyebrow. "So that tan meathead currently acting like my brother's best friend would be...?"

"A *friend* with odd timing and misplaced but good intentions," I finish.

Travis nods and sits down across from me.

"You hungry?" I ask him as I pick up the menu, needing a distraction.

He blinks and tilts his head, like he's not used to someone caring enough to ask him that question. "Yeah."

As if on cue, the server approaches.

"What can I get for you?" he asks, nervously eyeing Travis.

"I'll take a rum and coke," Travis says before looking at me.

"Do you have any food recommendations?" I ask the waiter.

"How hungry are you?"

I smile. "I could eat."

The older man looks to my companion. "You're a vegetarian, yes?" he clarifies.

Travis nods but doesn't withhold the surprise from his face.

"My daughter is a huge fan," the server explains bashfully.

"Oh, yeah?" Travis asks. "What's her name?"

"Gabby."

I can tell by his tone that he's really proud of her, and that makes me smile.

"She's in ninth grade," he adds.

"Was she at the show tonight?"

He grimaces as he shakes his head. "School night."

"Ah, right," Travis says. "If it were up to me, I'd only perform on the weekends, but the label very clearly disagrees."

The server laughs. "They make the rules. Well, for your dinner, I can personally vouch for the fig and goat cheese pizza as well as the panko-crusted tofu served with sauteed ginger and bok choy."

"Both of those sound perfect," I say. "If you don't mind sharing, Travis?"

He shrugs. "That's fine with me."

"I'll put that in for you," the man promises.

"Thanks," I tell him with a smile.

As I watch his retreating form, I notice a few curious gazes pointed our direction.

I'm not oblivious to the fanfare that surrounds Travis's every move. But I've been pretty shielded from it by hanging around backstage and being funneled through private entrances to buildings.

"How long did it take you to get used to it?" I ask him after a few minutes.

"What?" Travis asks, snapped out of his thoughts.

"Everyone knowing who you are." I point a finger in the air and clarify my wording. "Well, everyone knowing who you are and thinking they know *you*."

The corner of his mouth ticks. "The cameras and fans, I'm used to it by now. Thankfully, most hotels and venues now have hidden exits and plans in place to avoid the adoring mobs."

"I'm sure that helps."

"It does. Sometimes, I'll just be out to dinner with friends, and a stranger will approach the table asking for an autograph. That stuff still takes me by surprise, like I'm jarred out of normalcy."

"That's—"

"Hold that thought."

Travis pulls out his notebook as the server drops off his drink.

I can't see inside, but I watch him flip to a page and click his pen. "What are you writing?"

"'Jarred out of normalcy,'" he murmurs as the pen moves. "Okay."

"Is that what you write in there? Little snippets of conversation?"

He takes a sip of his drink and licks his bottom lip. "Sometimes."

"And what about other times?"

"Whatever inspires me in the moment," he says lowly, like it's a deep, dark secret.

And it might just be.

Aside from the words and lonely moments he has to himself, he's overexposed to the world.

I process this as our food arrives, and although it seems delicious, I can't appreciate the taste because I'm fixated on Travis—his every movement and learning what makes him tick.

To Dan's point earlier, I have been a little selfish.

My fleeting time spent in Travis's presence hasn't really contributed anything to our project other than background context and a few clips.

And, unfortunately, I need to remember what I'm here for.

"I really need you to sit down for an interview with

me," I say after swallowing a bite of delicious cheesy pizza.

"You know, I've read some of your work," Travis says instead of agreeing to anything.

"Really?" I ask, surprised at his deflection tactic.

"And most of the time, you reach out to the subject of the piece with a request to tell their side, and they always decline to comment," he says pointedly.

"Well, usually, my *subjects* are incarcerated or about to be the subject of an FBI investigation if they aren't already. You, however, are sitting in a restaurant tucked away in the most expensive hotel in the entire city of Denver and eating tofu. Right in front of a journalist."

He smirks. "So let's do it now."

I roll my eyes. "Of course, while Dan's preoccupied."

"What a shame."

With a sigh, I reach for my phone and adjust the settings on my camera, changing quality and frames per second in hopes I'll be able to get something usable enough for Dan to clean up in post-production.

"Ready?" Travis drawls as I try to use my purse to prop my phone up on the table.

"Almost," I murmur.

Across from me, Travis leans back, propping his foot up next to my thigh as he picks a piece of fig off the pizza and drops it in his mouth.

Most people aren't totally comfortable being interviewed, but Travis, of course, isn't most people.

He's totally unbothered, whether it's because he doesn't plan on answering any of my questions or because he's confident enough not to care, I'm not sure.

But I'd like to find out.

"Okay," I say, pressing the record button.

"Give me your best questions, Dakota," Travis orders. "None of that filler shit."

"So you don't want to talk about how excited you are to be talking with me today?" I tease.

He rolls his eyes. "Do I look excited?"

"I'm the one asking the questions here."

I earn a smile with that retort.

"What's one thing you wish you could do right now?" I ask.

"Eat my pizza without being asked questions," he answers promptly.

"Funny," I deadpan. "Seriously, though. Surely there's something in this world you would want to do if you were anonymous for one day. No secret entrances or people seeking autographs."

Travis takes a pull from his drink as he considers his response, and I take this as a good sign that he's not going to brush it off.

"I can't tell you how many cities I've been to. Or countries. For so long, I was so fucked up, drunk and high, that everything swirled together. Soundcheck. Do shots. Perform. Get some blow. Go out. Smoke a bit. Crash somewhere. Get shaken awake and stumble onto the plane or bus or whatever and do it all again. I've been so many places but never really *been* there, if that makes sense."

"It does," I encourage with a nod.

"I've just wasted a lot of time and opportunity," he says, clearly filled with regret. "What I wouldn't give to be that twenty-one-year-old kid again, for just one day. I was completely anonymous and could do anything I wanted. But instead, I chose to be overstimulated and unaware."

He stops and jots down that phrase in his notebook.

"No one wants to hear this shit, though," Travis continues, clicking his pen so it retracts. "No one feels bad for the rich and famous dude who's shattered on the inside and just needs a fucking break from it all."

"So that's what prompted your hiatus these past few years?" I ask, not without sympathy.

He laughs hollowly. "Is 'hiatus' the term people are using? I call it 'my personal life completely fell apart, and I needed to get my shit together before I could even think about getting back in the studio.'"

"And did it get put back together?"

"I'm working on it."

I rest my chin on my palm and appraise him. "So is that the reason behind the pivot of this album?"

"One of many. This is the last record on my current contract, and for an entire year, the label pressured me to, essentially, make a repeat of my first album. And I refused, straight-up stalling any meetings and hiding out until they listened to what I'd recorded so far and agreed on the direction. It took a long time to get to that point."

"Not off in rehab, then?" I pose, recalling what the gossip blogs speculated on.

He shakes his head. "I quit the drugs cold turkey, but the best therapy for me was just being at home and writing and singing the way I've wanted to."

"And do you feel you've accomplished that, finally?"

"In some ways." He pauses and takes a sip of his drink. "Do you remember when you were a kid or a teenager or whatever and you'd stay up late just because there was a novelty to it?"

"Yes," I say with a smile, intrigued where he's going with this. "I tried to stay up to see the sunrise so many times, but I never made it."

"Sunrise? You don't have to wait for sunrise, Dakota. Midnight is all you need. When the sky is so dark, it seems like it's a shade of blue, and you're enjoying the view of the stars without even knowing you've moved from one day to the next. But there's a new beginning clouded in that darkness. You just have to not let it pass by, and that's all I'm chasing now."

I smile at him slowly. "I think that was all worthy of your notebook."

He doesn't move to document any of it, choosing to simply stare at me with a look that's so intense, it actually makes me feel a little off.

I clear my throat, remembering we're recording. "So, is this the new direction you're going to be taking moving forward? This style."

"I don't know. I just wanted to end things on my own terms."

I blink. "What does that mean exactly? You're retiring?"

"Everything's still up in the air, but like I said, this is my last contracted record and tour with the label."

"But *Honest Chaos* is your best yet," I insist, taken aback. "And it's been your most well-received, critically. Not to mention all the sales records you're already breaking."

"Those are great footnotes for my Wikipedia page, but they don't really mean anything to me."

I don't buy his aloofness. "They're vanity metrics, but you're telling me it doesn't mean *anything* to you?"

He runs a hand through his hair. "It's nice to be liked. I don't think anyone would disagree with me there, but it's funny to me how people keep saying, like, 'Oh, this is a new chapter for Travis,' or whatever, but really, it's just me finally being able to produce what I've wanted to for years."

"So you're telling me you've had no creative control over anything, and you've been a victim of the system?" I scoff, doubling down. "I find that a little difficult to believe."

He shrugs, completely unbothered. "I'm not here to make you believe anything."

I look at him—*really* look past the rockstar exterior, overgrown hair, and blue eyes—and I can still somehow see that teenage boy from outside Pittsburgh, just trying to figure it all out.

My phone rings, interrupting our conversation, and we both see *MARK* flash on the screen.

It's not that action, exactly, that changes the dynamic between us, but I see how Travis clams up as he takes in the *very* not platonic contact picture I never got around to changing after we broke up.

I ignore the call and ensure that my and Travis's video recording is still intact.

"You kept this?" he asks, reaching for the Tootsie Pop that's sticking out of my purse.

"Yes," I say a little sheepishly.

His brow furrows slightly as he unwraps it. "No need to let it go to waste."

I'm frozen, watching how very innocently he brings it to

his lips, swiping the hard coated surface with his tongue before he sucks it in his mouth.

"Can I get either of you anything else?" the server asks.

"No, thank you," I say, voice a little hollow.

He nods and drops the check.

I break out of my stupor and reach for it, but Travis is faster, gripping it with one hand as he pulls his wallet out of his pocket with the other.

I should insist on paying, but the lines of ethics and boundaries are so skewed that I don't comment as I watch him pull a few hundred-dollar bills from his wallet—far exceeding the cost of our meal—then sign the back of the receipt "For Gabby" like it's absolutely nothing.

Once he's secured the gift under one of the plates in front of us, he gestures between me and my phone with the Tootsie Pop. "So, you and the guy…"

"Mark," I supply.

"You're done?"

I nod. "Totally and completely. Done. And just friends."

"Good."

"Yes."

And when he smiles at me, a full, wide grin with lips that are slightly stained blue, every single part of me wants a taste of him.

SIXTEEN

"You were just going to leave without saying goodbye?" Mark accuses playfully as he approaches me in the hotel lobby the next morning. "No goodbye call, text, or hug?"

"I'm surprised you're still standing," I retort. "You do recall drunk-dialing me multiple times last night, right?"

"I do," he says, dropping his voice. "Because I wasn't as blackout drunk as Devin was or thought me to be. You'd be surprised what information he spilled."

I glance around, ensuring I don't recognize anyone within earshot. "Like what?"

"Everything and nothing," he says cryptically. "But it's the little details that matter, Dakota."

"Uh-huh."

"He's *jealous* of Travis."

I roll my eyes. "Anyone with two working eyes and a brain could have figured that one out. Your skills are getting rusty, Mark."

He shakes his head. "It's more than that. The way he

talks about Travis's shift in direction lately is pretty resent-ful. More than just brotherhood rivalry."

That gives me pause.

Mark continues on in my silence. "Just remember that a manager, regardless of how bogus that job title is when it refers to him, is in charge of contracts and negotiation. It might be worth trying to get your hands on the latest version of those docs."

"This is a documentary about *Travis*. I'm not here to investigate Devin Young and whatever shady shit he's up to."

"Well, if it directly impacts the subject of your docu-mentary, isn't that a part of the job?" he argues.

"Less than a day ago, you were convinced Travis and I were carrying on some sort of love affair, based on our acting in one music video, and now you're trying to convince me to look after him?" I summarize with a little exasperation.

Mark shrugs. "Look, I'm just aiming to help you in the ways that I can. It doesn't make up for everything, not even close, but I'm trying."

I pull him in for a hug. "I know. And thank you."

"And for flying out here?" he teases.

I snort and pull back. "Definitely not."

"Well, I'm going to stick around here for a few days," he says. "You're off to Portland next, right?"

"Yep. Then Seattle, where Travis is headlining the music festival up there, and then there's a three-day break before we're due in Vancouver, then Chicago and a bunch of other cities in the Midwest and on the East Coast, and then Dan and I head back to New York to take up residence in the editing room."

"Busy girl," he notes, sticking his hands in his pockets.

"Always."

"Well, maybe I'll see you at Christmas." He tries and fails to suppress his sheepish smile.

"Mark, we talked about this," I remind him. "We need a break. Like a real, semi-permanent one."

He nods. "I heard you, loud and clear. But I feel obligated to mention that private detectives without the ex-boyfriend discount are pricier than you'd imagine. You know, just in case that changes things."

"I appreciate the sentiment," I say evenly. "But I'm sure I'll do just fine."

"I know you will."

I sigh and let him pull me in for a final hug.

He inhales and releases me. "Take care of yourself, Dakota."

"You too, Mark."

It really does feel like a firm goodbye this time.

There's a minuscule part of me that mourns the finality of it all, but I still resolve to push ahead, climbing into the van that's going to take us to the airport.

I'm the first in, as usual.

It's almost like clockwork now, how Leigh steps up, smiling brightly as she chats with Dan before they take their seats.

Then there's a roar of fanfare as Travis exits the hotel with his sunglasses on and his hood up. He does indulge a few requests for selfies before he climbs into the back of the vehicle, visibly relaxing at the shield the darkened windows offer.

Phoenix and Nick come next, signing a few autographs on their way as well, and since they're talking as they go, I assume they've come to some sort of truce to be able to exchange words without shouting.

Finally, after the duo, Devin practically rolls into the front seat, sipping Gatorade and complaining about how loud the fans are until he falls asleep.

We do it all over again when we get to the plane, and while I never expected to have a "spot" on a private jet, here we are.

I've learned that I'm less jittery if I distract myself. I focus all my attention on some silly word game app, but I'm not unaware of Travis's every move, half-listening to him talk to Leigh in low tones.

Once we're safely high enough in the sky that I can access the internet, I log into one of my social media accounts.

I've deliberately not kept up with much of the chatter on the Ellison piece while in this Travis Young bubble. I wanted to avoid the majority of the frustration and slight helplessness I feel about the situation, story, and lawsuit, but now that I have a little bit of time and nothing else to do, I scroll through my mentions and notifications.

As expected, there are a bunch of trolls—likely paid by Wall Street cronies—who tear apart my reporting and declare it all to be "fake news," in their support of Roger Ellison.

But there are a number of follow-up articles by the traditional media outlets, and I'm only slightly irked to see that Bryan is quoted talking about the story instead of me.

I'm not mad about missing out on the attention because, frankly, I'd rather not be in the spotlight, but I practically made this story my religion for almost a year, and Bryan's answers leave something to be desired.

There's nothing I can do about it now other than send him a bitchy email, but as good as it will feel in the moment to write it up, I know it won't matter. The major coverage of it is already gone, and I've missed my chance to ride the wave.

Part of me itches to open my document of notes and start thinking through the follow-up article, allowing my brain to dive right back into where I left off.

But I don't.

It's not just because I'm still devastated that *Exos* has taken me off the story as they sort out the legalities of the libel case but I really do need to finish up this whole documentary project, put it out in the world, and collect a check that's going to do amazing things for my credit cards and savings accounts.

Then, after all that, I can go back to my routine, where there's no paparazzi waiting around every corner, no gigantic bowl of green Skittles, and no sideways glances from tattooed musicians.

"You with me, Dakota?" Dan asks, pulling me from my thoughts.

I blink and refocus on Nick, who is clipping on his microphone as he settles on the bed in his hotel suite.

It takes me a second to come back to earth in our hotel in Portland because I've been so lost in my own thoughts.

I clear my throat and ready myself to play the part of a perfect interviewer. "Yes," I tell him. "We're good."

Dan puts on his headphones and gives me a thumbs-up.

I offer Nick a smile. "Can you tell me about when you first met Travis?"

"Sure," he says easily, unfazed by the camera that's picking up his every word. "I attended an open audition for a bassist, and I had no idea when I walked into the room that I would find Travis and Leigh and a bunch of label executives sitting inside."

He chuckles at his own recollection, then gives us the play-by-play of their first jam session. He also confesses that he was so nervous when they recorded together for the first time, his hands were sweaty, and he kept messing up.

Ultimately, we wrangle a few stories out of him that portray Travis as a perfectionist about his music—especially on this latest album—before we switch to lighter topics like funniest fan moments and the disaster of Travis's guitar getting stolen off a commercial flight.

When Phoenix hears we've successfully gotten Nick's take on Travis and their years together, he decides he's available for a sit-down too, so the next day, on the plane ride up to Seattle, we get about twenty minutes to drill him with questions.

It's a relief how much footage we now have to choose from, but it won't be until our days off after the festival that we'll start splicing the bones of the documentary together and see what we're missing. We've got a ton of B-roll and interviews from everyone around Travis, and—

I blink, realizing I never shared the footage of my talk with Travis.

It wasn't an intentional move on my part to deliberately hide it from Dan, but now, thinking through handing it over, I'm not sure I want to.

And that makes my stomach sink.

As we stop in traffic on the way to the music festival, I turn my head toward Travis and am startled to find that he's looking at me. The expression on his face is pensive, with his eyebrows pulled together and lips pursed.

He all but ignored me yesterday—something that disappointed me more than it should have—and I'm a little uncomfortable with how the line between reporting and personal conversations seems to have dissipated.

I'm out of my element for many reasons on this assignment, but even if I'm expected to have a closer relationship with my subject than normal, I definitely want to rewatch the footage to make sure it's…I don't know.

Ethical?

Moral?

Not embarrassing?

"Holy shit," Devin says, startling me.

I fix my gaze out the window again as we wind up close to the venue. The crowd is massive, and the line stretches out as far as I can see.

"Doors aren't even open for two hours," Devin says incredulously.

I find it surprising he actually knows that information.

"I expected this to be tiny."

"Tiny?" Leigh echoes in disbelief. "Seattle's a major city!"

Devin snorts. "I know, but this isn't exactly Coachella."

"Do you know *anything* about the music history here?" Nick snaps, unable to hide the annoyance in his tone.

"Yeah, I get it, still hanging onto Nirvana," Devin says with a dismissive wave of his hand. "It was, like, decades ago. Move on."

Nick holds his hand up to his heart, like he's been wounded, and Phoenix snickers.

"Wow," Leigh drawls before turning to Travis. "Now that we're here, there's actually something I wanted to talk to you about."

He rubs his eyes, then his temples. "What are you going to make me do that I don't want to?"

"A *very* quick interview with local media here tomorrow morning," she rushes out. "I could get you out of it, but please don't make me. It'll be fifteen minutes, max."

"Leigh," Travis sighs.

"Normally I wouldn't ask," she presses. "But a friend called in a favor."

When he still doesn't relent, she frowns.

"Remember how I got that *Vice* tell-all story suppressed a few years back?"

"Vaguely," he admits sourly.

"I'm going to pretend I didn't hear that," I mumble, hoping that I'll never have any part of my stories controlled in that way.

Leigh frowns. "Well, that reporter is now married to one of the producers, and this is them officially cashing in on the favor."

"Isn't the point of them—" Travis gestures to Dan and me. "—being here that they have the exclusive?"

"Oh, no," I jump in, offering him a sly grin. "Don't pass

up the opportunity on my behalf. It would actually be good to get some shots of you in that setting."

"Come on, Travis," Leigh pouts. "Please?"

"Fine," he relents.

But I have a feeling that it will not, in fact, be fine.

And I'm right.

The day continues on normally enough, except they're playing at an outdoor venue for the first time on this tour, which means instead of a spacious backstage area, we're all shoved into one RV that serves as both a dressing room and a green room.

Surprisingly, Travis isn't headlining the festival, but he is the act just as the sun starts to set.

It's a little weird to watch him play not under the total cover of darkness, but I don't mind seeing him shine in the light when the band does finally go on.

I've heard the set enough times that not only do I know every single line to each song but I'm starting to pick up on the little errors in timing or notes played. The audience remains oblivious, but Nick's backup vocals on one song are a little off-key, and Phoenix is just a tad out of sync with Travis's guitar part on another.

At first, it seemed a little nitpicky to me that Travis got frustrated by that kind of stuff, but now I understand him enough to know that it's not about perfection, necessarily, but ensuring that his creativity and vision are brought to life the right way.

I can read him much better now, so I practically feel his growing irritation until he stops singing mid-bridge of "The Belated Death of White Fairy Dust."

I gasp at the interruption.

Travis stomps over to the front of the stage and starts yelling into the crowd, gesturing wildly.

I can't pick up his words at first, so I step forward, just in front of the curtain, to see what all the fuss is about.

Some glassy-eyed guy holds up his hands defensively as he argues with Travis, while most of the crowd loudly boos at the break in the performance.

"Don't fucking touch her," Travis growls into the microphone, still staring down at the guy. "She's drunk and uninterested, and you're a scumbag."

"Fuck you, you washed-up piece of shit," the guy yells loud enough that even I can hear.

Four hulking security guards dressed in all black descend on the scene.

But Travis is faster, throwing off his guitar and jumping down to continue verbally sparring with the guy, pushing the crying girl at the root of the argument behind him and out of the way.

Dan runs on the stage—something he's never once done before—to capture the moment Travis successfully lands a punch. He's immediately pulled back by two of the guards as the other two throw out the creep.

The crowd loses it, cheering Travis on as the guards release him and he jumps back on the stage, yelling at the offender until he's completely out of sight.

His chest heaves with adrenaline, and I can't pull my eyes away from how utterly wild he looks at this moment.

"Now that that's taken care of, let's get back to it," he yells, gripping the microphone stand.

The screams of the crowd are louder than I've ever heard them.

Travis nods to Nick, then Phoenix, and they pick up right where they left off, totally in sync.

"Travis," Leigh says, appearing beside me. "This is going to cause a PR nightmare."

"For the right reasons, though," I offer.

She frowns. "I know, but I've seen how these things play out. People will spin anything to get a story."

I nudge her with my elbow. "Then it's a good thing I'm here to report the truth."

"Yeah," she says, but her word lacks confidence.

SEVENTEEN

Dan and I tag along with Leigh and Travis for the interview.

I'm curious to see with my own eyes how Travis interacts with another reporter, but Dan is just gleeful at getting more footage of Travis where he's not practically shirtless in front of thousands of adoring fans.

In fact, this is the most dressed up I've seen Travis.

He's wearing a pair of jeans without holes in them, for once, and a short-sleeved, button-up shirt that barely reveals any of his tattooed chest.

I've become so accustomed to seeing the ink that I can't help but miss it just a little bit.

When we arrive at the small offices of the local media outlet—making *Exos* feel massive in comparison—we're immediately escorted to a small room that's been converted to a studio.

The camera operator directs Travis to sit in front of a green screen, which is an odd choice, given the nice framing in the windows we passed by in the hallway, but I keep my mouth shut.

I guess I've learned more about the video process than I've realized these past few weeks.

"Leigh Baker, you're a vision," the forty-something interviewer says as he glides into the room.

She smiles flatly. "It's good to see you, Jim."

"And Dakota Shaw, it's truly an honor to meet you. That story you did last year on the mayoral candidate's collusion with big oil...all I can say is wow." He beams at me, then turns to Travis and settles in on the chair beside him. "And of course, the man of the hour...year...decade."

I quirk a brow at Leigh, who shrugs as we get the signal that the camera is rolling.

"I'm so happy to have the chance to sit down with you," Jim says. "It's been a while since you've given an interview."

Travis nods but doesn't say anything.

"How have you been?" Jim asks.

"Good," Travis answers noncommittally as he shifts in his chair.

To the untrained eye, his one-word answer comes off as arrogant, like he's too big to indulge this interviewer.

But I'm floored to realize he's actually uncomfortable.

Or maybe even nervous.

That idea seems ridiculous because he played in front of forty thousand people last night.

"It's been a few years since you've been back in Seattle," Jim prompts.

"I think so, yeah."

The interviewer glances down at his notes, which I find

a little odd, given that he's asked only the most basic questions thus far.

It might be a deliberate tactic on his part, asking softball questions to open him up, but I think he'd have more luck if he asked something open-ended.

"And how does it feel to be back?"

Travis shifts again, tapping his foot on the floor. "The crowds here have always been good to me, and there's something pretty cool about playing in a city with such important music history."

Jim smiles, seeming pleased enough with that soundbite. "Let's talk about your music."

Travis runs a hand through his hair but doesn't speak.

Undeterred, Jim tells him, "This album in particular has been well received."

"So I'm told," Travis says flippantly.

His remark could be read as a snub to his fans, who continuously flood his social channels with comments of support, or it might make him come off as totally conceited.

"You haven't kept up with what people are saying?" Jim asks curiously. "Too busy partying and celebrating? After all, you've got quite a reputation—"

"No," Travis says quickly. "I've been clean for years. I'm at the stage of my life and my career where I just want to focus on the music."

"Fair enough," Jim says, leaning into his friendly tone. "But I'd like to get some of your off-the-cuff reactions to the coverage. That okay with you?"

Travis looks just beyond the camera, to Leigh, with an annoyed glance.

She rolls her eyes and nods, encouraging him to play along and get this over with.

"Sure," Travis says to Jim, straining to keep his voice even.

It's barely been five minutes since the interview started, and it's already a train wreck.

Jim rifles through some papers on his lap. "I have a few tweets here, but this one is my favorite. 'I want to have sex with Travis Young's new album.'"

Travis snorts. "I guess I'll take that as a compliment."

"Another person asks if they could pay double the ticket price for one of your shows to be spit on by you."

"Pass, but thanks for the offer," Travis quips as he crosses his arms on his chest.

Leigh pinches the bridge of her nose.

Jim chuckles. "Well, this one is from a music critic, which is far less vulgar but a little more on the negative side."

"Great," Travis says sarcastically.

"'Travis Young tried something with this new album. *Tried* being the key word. Didn't say he *succeeded*.'"

There's a moment of silence as the camera operator pans to Travis, waiting for some sort of explosion, but he only chews his bottom lip as he lets the words roll off him.

"Okay, then," Travis says finally.

"You don't have a comment on that?" Jim nudges. "No thoughts or objections or anything to say in response?"

I know why he's harping on this, but that doesn't mean it's easy to watch.

It's all the more reason I stick to investigative reporting, which is all based on facts and events, not subjective opinions.

Jim is hoping to derail Travis, who is notorious for making headlines, and use it to either promote himself or his publication.

Travis, to his credit, doesn't even flinch. "No comment."

"Have you heard that before?" Jim asks.

"Nope."

"So you don't read anything people say about you online. Positive or negative?"

Travis's jaw ticks. "I didn't say that. But I'm not exactly interested in that particular opinion."

"You don't care about what the public says about your pretty radical shift in direction?"

"It's not that I don't care." Travis pauses, choosing his words carefully. "Look, I spent *years* writing these songs. Agonizing over every word. Being meticulous as hell about the chords and melody and all that shit, only for someone to come in and say something dismissive like that? It's not worth my time, really."

Jim nods and leans forward, zeroing in on Travis. "So you don't like to be criticized?"

"It's not the criticism," Travis argues. "It's the delivery."

"Not a fan of social media?"

"What I mean is that art is open to interpretation. I know I'm not for everyone, and I'm not trying to be. I don't make music for anyone but myself."

"Well, I'm sure your fans will *love* to hear that."

Travis narrows his eyes. "I'd hope that after all this time, my fans would support my music because they enjoy it, not suddenly abandon it because some critic doesn't understand what I'm trying to do."

"Have you ever heard the phrase, 'Don't bite the hand that feeds you,' Travis?" Jim muses.

Travis laughs hollowly. "That's about enough."

Leigh sighs beside me but doesn't look all that surprised.

Travis stands up and tears off his microphone. "I'm done with this shit, dude."

"Wait up," Jim implores innocently. "We were just talking."

Travis ignores him as he frowns at Leigh. "Sorry," he says as he walks out. "I tried."

Jim looks to the camera, smiles, and shrugs, like he has no idea what could have caused Travis to walk out of the conversation.

Leigh, despite understanding Travis's reaction, steps in to do damage control. "Well, I think you got some usable stuff in there."

Dan lowers his camera and grins at me, happy to have stumbled on another gold nugget of content in the past twenty-four hours.

For the sake of the documentary, I probably should be thrilled at the turn of events, but my first and last thoughts are of Travis.

How many times has he been subjected to something like this?

I'd be tired, too, if I went through what he did and had someone imply there's nothing more to being a rockstar than partying.

And I guess I'm "lucky" enough that I don't have to

interact with my critics face-to-face, whereas Travis has to deal with people giving him their unwanted opinions and takes on his words, on top of dealing with fame, photographers, and very excited fans.

It doesn't help that everyone around him is in relation to his career.

I can imagine sometimes he just needs a real friend or at least someone who wants to be with him with no other motive than to enjoy his presence.

And so purely on instinct, I go after him.

My limbs move, chasing Travis down like they're compelled to do so, and I can't decide if I want to reassure him or if I just selfishly want to be around him.

Travis is about six inches taller than me, which means his strides are far longer than mine, so I jog to catch up.

Even then, I'm barely able to slide in beside him before the elevator door closes.

Turning to face him, I try to be subtle about how out of breath I am while also silently giving thanks that I put on a pair of comfortable loafers today instead of heels.

His sunglasses are firmly in place, reflecting my own frown back at me.

"Are you okay?" I ask.

He sighs and jabs the button for the lobby. "Did Leigh send you after me?"

"No."

"Then why are you following me?"

I swallow, wishing I could see his eyes. "Do you remember the other day at the bar? What you said to me about not really getting to *see* all the places you go?"

He nods.

I take a deep breath, letting the air fill my lungs before I expel it, trying to let go of all the tension.

"Well, I've never been to Seattle before. And I was thinking...maybe you haven't seen it really or done it right. Visited all the spots that everyone talks about." I stop to collect myself before I take the next leap. "I figure, if all the music snobs are going to be at the festival, maybe you'd want to go be a tourist in the city with me?"

I'm almost proud that I sound more confident than I feel.

Travis works his jaw. "As you can tell, I'm not really in the mood to be interviewed today, Dakota."

"No interviews," I say earnestly. "Just us."

He pulls out his notebook as the elevator dings and the doors open on the first floor.

I crane my neck as we walk and watch him jot down the two words I just said aloud before he shoves it back into his pocket to await the next moment of inspiration.

As we exit the building, he puts his hand on my lower back to steer me away from the people on the sidewalk. For once, there are no photographers or screaming fans in sight, and we maneuver with relative ease.

"So, what do you want to do first?" Travis asks.

I smile up at him as I register how hopeful he sounds, like he's trying to temper his excitement at the prospect of simply enjoying the day ahead.

I reach for my phone, intending to search for something to do, but my gaze scans our surroundings and catches on a famous Seattle building not too far from where we stand.

"How about the Space Needle?" I suggest, gesturing over to it.

"Works for me," Travis says.

We head off in that direction, and I'm more than happy to walk beside Travis as he decompresses.

I think part of spending time with someone means being okay with the quiet in the moments when one of you just needs to let your mind breathe.

With each step, frustration and anger leave his body. It's like the farther we get away from Leigh and that disaster of an interview, the more he can let it go.

His arms become more pliable, and when we buy our tickets at the kiosk, his spine isn't held as rigidly.

And by the time we step into the elevator to the top of the structure, he's at ease enough to offer me a small smile.

"Can you take our picture?" an older woman asks Travis.

I have to withhold my laughter at his surprise, and I find myself wondering if he's ever been asked to photograph someone else instead of being photographed himself.

"Sure," he agrees, holding the woman's phone and taking a number of pictures at a few different angles as their entire family crowds together.

"Thank you so much," she says, beaming at the snaps he took. "Do you want me to take one of the two of you?"

I shake my head. "No, that's—"

"Do you mind?" Travis interjects, unlocking his phone and handing it over to her with a smile.

"Of course not," she says.

Travis slides his arm around my shoulders, pulling me closer to him at the same second that the elevator starts its ascent, and I almost fall over, but he holds me steady in his grasp.

"Smile!" the woman urges us as she taps the capture button.

"Thanks," Travis says gratefully, taking his phone back.

The tour guide tells us a little bit about what we're seeing through the windows as we move upward, but I'm barely listening because I'm still pulled against his chest.

"Let's see how she did," Travis says as he angles his phone screen toward me.

He flips through the images, and at least half of them have the woman's thumb over the lens, which cracks us both up.

We try to hold in our laughter, but it's always hard not to laugh in situations where you're decidedly not supposed to—like when someone is giving a very passionate spiel about the history of the Emerald City.

But when both doors open, we finally let it out as we're ushered out and down to the impressive observation deck. Our residual chuckles eventually wear off as we both take in the view of the city and the water.

We're given three-hundred-sixty-degree views around the structure, and one part of the floor is completely made of thick glass, so we can see straight down to the entrance and street below.

"So it's just planes you're afraid of?" Travis asks in amusement as I stare at the little dots of people hundreds of feet beneath us. "Not heights in general?"

"I think I'm getting better at planes," I tell him.

"The nervous grip marks on your seat say otherwise."

He's not entirely wrong.

I scowl at him playfully. "Yes, it's planes specifically. I've spent countless hours researching the mechanics of flying and researching how planes work—"

"Of course you have."

"But I still can't wrap my head around it. There are thousands of parts moving together all at once and somehow shoot wind through fast-moving fans and hurl humans into the air."

"That makes sense," Travis agrees.

"I do like the phrase 'airbreathing jet engines,' though," I admit, recalling some of the vocabulary I picked up along the way. "You should write that down."

"You don't get a say in what goes in my notebook," he argues, even as he takes it out to scribble them in.

"I appreciate facts and logic, okay?" I laugh and gesture to the glass floor. "For instance, even though this is a bit of an optical illusion, I can easily convince myself I'm not going to fall to my death because it's structurally sound."

To prove my point, I take a step onto the pane, even though my stomach lurches slightly, and hold out my hand for him to come join me.

"I'm not sure my brain works the same way yours does," he hedges, admiring the view of the street below from the safety of the carpeted area.

"Well, obviously," I say. "Mine hasn't been clouded with years of fame and fortune."

"Mean, Dakota."

"Come on," I say, wiggling my fingers. "It's less effort than punching a concert-goer in the face."

"Well, when you put it that way..." He accepts my grasp and keeps his eyes locked on mine as he steps forward, knees shaking just a bit.

"This is a mindfuck," he says, glancing down at our feet.

"So is life," I shrug.

"Touché."

Travis and I continue to wander around the circular structure, still hand in hand, and we spend at least twenty minutes simply watching the city from up above, marveling as a few planes come in and land on the water.

He finally drops my grasp to pull out his notebook again, and although I immediately feel the loss, his words make up for it.

No clouds in sight
At this new height
With you

EIGHTEEN

It starts out innocently enough.

With my map app as our guide, we walk through the city. Our destination is Pike Place, the bustling, open-air market right by the water, but I'm just enjoying the route that takes us there.

After spending so many years in New York, this city feels quaint and comfortable to me. There are still things I recognize from home, like cabs, public transportation, little fenced-off parks, and plenty of foot traffic.

It's like the convenience of Manhattan had a baby with the trendiness of Brooklyn.

And, of course, seeing it all with Travis heightens the experience.

We pass interesting groups of people, shops, and restaurants, and I ask his opinion on every little thing, curious to see what kind of food he likes and which experiences he recalls from being here in the past.

He gets stopped twice for autographs and photos, and

although it's still odd to me how normal it is for him to be approached by random people, it doesn't seem to weigh him down at all.

He does, however, lead me into a very touristy shop to buy a hat, using it to cover his hair in hopes of being less recognizable, then insists on getting me a matching beanie and scarf.

"If I'm going to look like an asshole, you're going to join me," he reasons.

I quirk an eyebrow. "Am I?"

He nods. "It's part of the tourist experience that you promised me today."

I relent and let him carefully place the accessories on me, and after a swipe of his credit card, we're off again.

The sidewalk in front of the original Starbucks in Pike Place is packed, so we detour up the cobblestone street to scope out a place where we can fuel up for more exploring.

The more populated area forces us to close the friendly distance between us, and although we already held hands up on the Space Needle, every little touch from Travis somehow sears my skin beneath the fabric of my dress.

While we stand in line for a promising little French bakery, his palm gently rests on my lower back as he looks at the beautiful pastries and macarons in the display case. It's such a ridiculously innocent gesture, but it makes me feel giddy.

This is the moment, really, when the touching starts between us.

It's nothing inappropriate, but it feels more friendly than we've been.

As we mill around, sampling honey and apple slices

from vendors, his hands are always somewhere on me—my waist, my shoulders, my back. There are so many little movements that I can hardly pay attention to anything else around me.

We whiz by gorgeous flower arrangements and stop with the flow of foot traffic as other pedestrians want a closer look at a booth.

At one point, I'm yanked back, my back flush against Travis's chest, as a man stumbles and narrowly avoids crashing into me. I glance up at Travis in shock, only to be reminded how *tall* and imposing he is, and wish he was visibly as off-kilter as I feel.

"Come on," he says, encouraging me forward with his hands on my hips. "This looks cool."

My legs are like jelly, but somehow, I get them to cooperate enough to move through the double doors leading to a wooden pier. There are a few stalls set up selling food, but we move toward the edge, inhaling the scent of fresh, sea air.

Travis pulls up his phone, trying to get his bearings and figuring out where the aquarium and the Great Wheel are before he points out the approaching ferry cutting across the water.

I think it's cool that in New York, you can take a train to a beach and feel like you've been transported to a different place, but here, the city seems to be just as much a part of local life as does the mountain I'm currently taking in.

"Beautiful," I say, watching the clouds shift to provide an even clearer view of Mt. Rainer. "I haven't done much hiking, but that looks intimidating."

"I did some hiking when I was at home last summer," he says. "Mostly trails and wooded areas. I really liked it."

I glance over at him. "I can't picture you as the outdoorsy type."

"Maybe someday I will be." He shrugs. "It's therapeutic, honestly. Being outside and out of cities and planes and whatnot."

I nod. "I can understand the appeal of that."

"So many years of my life have flown by so quickly, and really, Dakota, I'm just trying to slow down." He props his elbows on the ledge and leans on them. "Seattle is almost always on the tour list, and since Washington was one of the first states to legalize weed, that was how I spent most of my time here. Smoking it up in a van before getting wasted at a bar."

I turn away from the sight and take in his contemplative demeanor. "What changed?"

"I got arrested." Travis looks at me dead-on, piercing me with his blue eyes. "People tend to talk about their 'rock-bottom' moment. Thankfully, I don't think I ever reached that level, but I got pretty damn close."

"So that's when you quit?" I ask.

He nods. "The cop who arrested me hates my guts, and honestly, it's for good reason. I've had a few encounters with him over the years, and I've spent a lot of my life acting like an entitled little shit. So he pushes for the maximum penalty on anything I get busted for and even lobbies to get bonus charges added in."

"I've seen the records," I remind him.

"Right. Well, getting dragged through the court system for years isn't ideal, and neither is jail time, obviously, but this judge took pity on me. Instead of the years behind bars Officer Jackass was pressing for, I was only slapped with court-mandated rehab, house arrest, community service, and a long probation period. I don't take it for granted, but I do know it recalibrated my brain in a way."

"Sounds exhausting."

"It was," Travis agrees.

"But it's good that you did all that and came out better on the other side."

"It's also nice to not be high out of my mind all the time," he adds. "Experiencing these past few shows without snorting or smoking beforehand has helped me stay hyper-focused on what I want to do after the tour is over."

"So, you're using this one final hurrah to transition into something better?" I ask.

"Kind of."

"And you're okay with that?"

Travis quirks a brow. "Isn't that what you're doing, too?"

"I don't know," I tell him. "In some ways, it doesn't really feel like I'm doing much of anything."

"What do you mean?" he balks. "You've been hounding everyone about interviews nearly nonstop since we landed on the West Coast. Every single time I look at you, you're jotting down notes."

"Well, you must not be looking at me very often, then," I argue.

I watch the smirk form on his lips.

"Oh, I am," he says slowly, almost dangerously.

And those words do something to me that I'm not quite ready to unpack.

"For a reporter, you're not that stealthy, Dakota," he continues nonchalantly. "Openly gawking at me in public and trying to figure me out. And maybe you have, I don't know…I know you're good at what you do. But, not to give myself too much credit here, I know that's true because *I'm* good at what *I* do."

"What do you mean?"

"I don't just write songs and perform them. I observe life, situations, and little moments and then try to capture the art from it all and make it accessible to others who will never get to experience it."

He reaches into his pocket, pulls out his notebook, and then hands it over to me.

I blink up at him, astonished. "Really?"

"Really," he replies.

With shaking hands, I thumb through the pages.

Playing pretend.
Wishing it was real.

Under my skin.
More painful and permanent than a tattoo.

Is it selfish to want another person all to yourself?

Jealousy. Melancholy. Atrophy.

Cheers to another night of despair and loneliness and blonde hair.

I can't take anymore.

"Travis," is all I can say, and my voice isn't very strong.

The lines are so fucking blurred for this assignment, they might as well not even exist, and I don't have the emotional bandwidth or brain processing speed to vocalize anything I'm feeling.

"Come on," he says, shoving his notebook back in his pocket before he puts his arm around my shoulder.

It's as if we were made to do this whole walking with our limbs attached thing, perfectly matched to fit.

If we didn't move so easily together, I bet I would have stayed rooted to that spot, but I wonder what else we could do together.

What if Travis's calloused fingertips slipped down and caressed my skin?

Would his mouth be rough against mine, demanding everything I have, or would it be soft and warm, coaxing me slowly into him?

How would his tattoos taste if I traced them with my tongue?

"Car's on the way," he tells me.

All I can do is nod.

We have to cut back through the crowded interior of the market to get to our pickup spot, and in our time outside, the amount of people seems to have tripled.

And worse, it's no longer quiet locals doing their shopping or tour groups making a brief stop. It's a lot of young people dressed like we're back in the nineties, and they're much rowdier than I am prepared for.

"Holy shit, it's Travis Young!" someone in the crowd shrieks.

Travis swears under his breath but steels himself for the impending wave of teenagers pushing through to get to us.

But he doesn't remove his arm from my shoulder, managing to sign autographs with his nondominant hand as we continue to hurry toward the exit.

With each passing second, the attention on us grows, and more people line up for autographs.

There's an increasing number of phones and cameras being lifted into the air, and I step out from under Travis's arm, not wanting to be framed in the pictures that will absolutely make the rounds online.

Immediately, I'm shoved away by an overeager fan.

"Dakota!" Travis calls out when I stumble.

I barely catch myself as the pressure from the mob increases.

I turn to tell him I'm fine, but before I can speak, though, I see the murderous expression on his face.

He expertly removes himself from the crowd of fans, who are still shoving shirts and pieces of paper in his face to try to get an autograph, and comes to me, slipping his hands behind my legs and across my back.

He lifts me into his arms, as if I weigh absolutely nothing, and I don't fight the urge to fall into him, allowing him to cradle me closer as we ignore the people calling for him.

"The car's just up ahead," he murmurs to me. "On the next block."

Once the crowd has parted enough to let us through, I assure him, "I can walk."

"I know," he retorts but makes no move to let me down.

Frankly, I think this is a great deterrent for the group

who trail us, since having me in his arms makes it impossible for Travis to indulge their requests.

But one peek over his shoulder reveals that the majority of onlookers have simply switched to recording his every move.

I swallow the dread that comes with knowing those videos are going to be played on every gossip site, where witnesses will detail his whereabouts and readers will undoubtedly speculate about me.

I tuck my head against his shoulder, hiding from the cameras, and feel his chest move as I swear he sighs in relief at the way I give in.

He moves quickly toward the waiting black SUV, and the driver, seeing our approach, jumps out to open the door for us.

Travis nods at him and climbs in, still holding me to him.

Even once the door closes and we're safely hidden behind tinted windows, neither of us moves to untangle from the other.

NINETEEN

I find myself in Travis's hotel room under the guise of a drink.

It's a stretch, given that we haven't even had dinner yet, but it's a flimsy enough excuse for me to buy into it without hesitation, consequences be damned.

Well, I'm not so much *damning* them as pretending they don't exist for now.

Because the thought of not spending as much time as possible with Travis is almost unbearable at this point.

The room is ultra-modern and cool in the way only Seattle can be—industrial-chic but also high-tech. Travis sets the lights to a green-blue hue that feels romantic in a kind of punk-rock way.

After taking a moment to freshen up, I stare at myself in the mirror of his bathroom, hardly recognizing my reflection. I'm wearing the same old moderately professional clothes I normally do, and my hair is styled straight as usual, but there's something different about me that I can't put my finger on.

"Beer or whiskey?" Travis calls.

Hell, he could give me gasoline in a glass and I'd drink it.

I brace my hands against the marble countertop as that thought rolls through my head.

How the hell have I gotten in so deep?

I was supposed to go on the road, film some interviews, then get back to my life in New York.

Starting to fall for a goddamn rockstar was absolutely not on my checklist.

"What the hell am I doing here?" I whisper, taking in my slightly flushed skin as my heart thumps in my chest.

The version of me I still cling to, the bright-eyed, driven young reporter who was thrilled to get her start at *Exos*, would be so ashamed of where I am now.

And of what I want to do.

"Dakota?" Travis says, knocking on the door. "You okay?"

I rip the scarf off my neck and toss it beside the beanie on the counter, making it a little easier to breathe.

I should have never come up to this room.

I should have ignored the touches and the simmering heat between us.

I should have let him walk away from the interview alone and not chased after him.

And most of all, I shouldn't give in to opening that door.

But, of course, I do, and the reward is so sweet that my instincts practically scream at me for fighting them so hard.

Travis grips the ledge above the doorframe, appearing as if he is dangling before me.

His shirt crawls up, giving me an eyeful of his tattooed and taut abdomen, but that's not even the best part.

I've spent a lot of time today objectifying him, but the look of rawness on his face in this moment tugs at my heartstrings in a way that has logic temporarily overpowering my lust.

I don't think he does openness often, if at all, so if this is as close as I'm going to get, I'm going to appreciate it.

I step closer, holding his gaze, and the intensity I see there almost forces me to my knees. I stand tall and very delicately run my fingertips along his warm skin, tracing the lines of ink and muscle.

He shivers and renews his grip over my head, holding himself in place.

The fact that I'm able to make his breath hitch empowers me to continue. I move carefully upward, trying to memorize every single visible inch as I slowly unbutton his shirt.

Travis is patient, letting me explore and appreciate him until I pop the final button and drag my nails down from his collarbone to his belt buckle.

Then everything changes.

And I'm no longer in control.

Travis growls, then pivots and pushes my back flush against the wall.

I'm pinned with his thighs, locked in a gaze with his wild eyes.

My mouth is mere inches from his, and I'm aware we're both breathing somewhat raggedly.

"Dakota." My name is a plea on his lips. "Are you sure?"

He's giving me an out, understanding just as well as I do that this means something, and the next step will irrevocably change our time together.

Because Travis may normally be cool and calculated, but he doesn't half-ass anything.

He's meticulous about his music, fierce with his words, and serious as hell, and damn do I want to see him completely undone.

"Yes," I whisper.

It's the last coherent thought I have before our lips crash together, and I give into him completely.

Our rhythm is overwhelming in the best way.

I forget anything exists except Travis Young as he parts my lips with his tongue, and the pressure of our connection is so damn good, my entire body tingles.

Travis tangles one hand in my hair, exposing my neck for him to lick and suck, as the other trails up my spine, searching for the start to my dress's zipper.

Inch by inch, he tugs it down and exposes my skin. The fabric finally hits the floor, and I'm left panting as he swirls his tongue under the lace of my bra.

I sigh contentedly. "Travis."

He moves almost lazily as his hands and mouth explore me, and my entire body pulsates under his touch.

I clench my thighs together before rubbing myself against the straining denim of his jeans.

He practically hisses at the friction, and I have a fleeting thought that if the foreplay feels this good already, I can't imagine what it's going to be like when he's finally inside me.

Impatient to know the answer, I lift a leg, giving myself the leverage to grind my hips on his.

He jolts back and grins before recapturing my lips in a fast, bruising kiss, then he steps back, leaving me breathless.

"Fuck," he pants, pupils blown wide.

He tears his shirt off, letting it crumple to the floor, and I get an unobstructed view of how sculpted and decorated his skin is.

I want to ask him the backstory behind every single tattoo marring his skin, but I'm distracted by the sound of his belt unbuckling.

My gaze snaps up to his, and whatever expression is on my face makes him smile.

"Undress for me, Dakota."

I oblige without hesitation, holding his eyes as I unsnap my bra and toss it on top of the clothing pile.

As a reward, he kicks off his jeans, and my mouth waters at the sight of his erection straining against the material of his boxer briefs before they come off, too.

He sits back on the bed, content to enjoy the show I'm putting on for him.

I swallow as my fingers hook the edges of my thong and drag it down over my sensitive skin before kicking away the fabric.

Travis sharply inhales at the sight of me completely bare. "Come here," he demands.

I approach on shaking legs, and he pulls me down onto the bed, fixing himself on top of me.

His hands hold mine up against the pillows as our mouths meet, moving frantically together.

I'm pinned beneath him, our friction driving me wild, and judging by the way he drives his thigh against my clit, he knows it.

"Travis," I moan between gritted teeth.

As a matter of pride, I'm not one to ask for favors, even the sexual kind, but all I want is for him to touch me.

And I wouldn't mind begging for it.

He chuckles as he moves his fingers down at a slow pace, but I grow frustrated, break from his grasp, and slide my hand down to the apex of my thighs.

I rub myself with my middle finger while Travis rests on his elbows, watching how my hips rock into the movement. With my other hand, I palm his erection.

It's erotic as hell to do this with him watching me.

He moans and bats my hands away, kissing me again, first on my lips and then on my nipples before he fishes a condom from his wallet—and, to my surprise, his little notebook, which he drops on the nightstand.

He tears open the packet and rolls the condom on.

I don't want to give him the upper hand here because I know what I need to finish, and I don't have time to build up to it.

I need him inside me.

Now.

I press my hands to his chest, first pushing him back and then keeping him still as I swing a leg over his body to position myself on top of him. I let out a moan as I start to sink down on the head of his cock, moving slowly as I adjust to his size.

"Dakota," he hisses as he bottoms out inside me.

I start rocking back and forth, nearly coming apart as I do.

He doesn't lie back and take it, though. He throws me slightly off-balance as he sits up, peppering kisses on my mouth, neck, and breasts as I move, and he surges upward with each thrust.

I dig my fingernails into his skin, holding on but building to let go. We move together, our tongues and limbs, until we both come apart—me first, then him.

In the aftermath, we lie panting, sweaty and in pure bliss.

Moments pass, and then he reaches over to the nightstand for his notebook and jots down words for me to see.

Lay entangled, finally.

He checks the time as he drops it back on the nightstand, then smiles at me. "Dakota."

"Travis," I say as I roll closer to him, placing my hand on his chest just because I can.

"It's almost midnight, and I want to show you something."

I can practically *feel* his earnestness. "Okay," I give in.

Travis slides on his jeans while I don my bra and thong, but I frown at the thought of putting my crumpled dress back on.

"Here," he says, tossing me a shirt from his suitcase.

I slip it on over my head, grateful to find it hits me mid-thigh. "Thanks."

"Come on," he says, offering me a hand.

I eye my bare legs and his lack of a shirt. "Where are we going?"

"You'll see," he says with a crooked smile that toes the line of being a know-it-all smirk.

We hastily slip into the hotel-supplied slippers, and he leads us out of the room and into the elevator.

"Pool's closed," I note, reading the sign as he pushes the button for the rooftop.

"If there's ever a perk of being who I am, Dakota, it's that rules don't apply to me."

I roll my eyes and smile. "Your probation begs to differ."

"Point taken." He drips a kiss on the tip of my nose. "Let me clarify, then, and say that *some* rules don't apply to me. And this is one of them."

I don't argue with the confidence he exudes as we step out on the rooftop, and he leads me over to the edge.

We take in the sight of the city at night, the lights of the buildings around us and in the ships in the water, and it's fucking *magical*.

I never thought I would feel like this or even exist in this way with a man I'm starting to have terrifyingly strong feelings for in such a short time, and it's almost daunting to accept that this is real life.

I exhale as he brushes my hair over my shoulder.

"You remember when you told me that you've always wanted to stay up until sunrise?" Travis asks me.

"And you said midnight was all I needed."

I pause and take in the marvelousness of the half-asleep city that somehow still feels charged, even at this hour.

"I can appreciate your argument even more now, I think. There *is* a new beginning clouded in darkness."

"You can't just let it pass you by," he finishes, sliding his thumb along my bottom lip.

When I reach up and press my hand against his beating heart, he laces our fingers together, holding our grasp to his sternum like it's giving him life.

And I realize with complete certainty that I could jump in the private jet right now and fly to any destination in the world—and absolutely nothing would feel as complete to me as the sight of Travis Young at midnight.

TWENTY

I didn't have one single sip of alcohol yesterday, but when I wake up, I feel hungover because being with Travis is intoxicating.

My phone has been buzzing for the last ten minutes, but I've been pretending it doesn't exist.

Once I open my eyes to the morning light, I'm going to have to face reality, and I much prefer my current situation with Travis's arms locked around my waist.

But the sound doesn't stop, so I sigh as I surrender and squint at my phone screen, only to sit up abruptly when I read the text message from Dan freaking out over where the hell I am.

I'm an hour late to the all-day editing session that he and I have planned, and I have no excuse.

"Shit," I mutter as I jump up and try to remember where I left my shoes.

"Dakota," Travis groans as he rolls over and finds my side of the bed empty.

"I'm so late," I tell him, trying to decide if I can get away with just wearing his shirt to dash down the hall to my room or if I should slip on my dress.

Walking around the hotel in this state didn't seem like an issue under the cover of darkness, but now I feel over-exposed.

"Come back to bed," he protests, sitting up to reveal his adorably messy and sexy bedhead. "We can order room service."

My stomach growls at the thought because I'd love nothing more than to stay in bed with Travis and enjoy a massive breakfast.

But all those consequences I ignored last night are proverbially smacking me in the face right now in the form of text messages.

I reluctantly slip off his shirt and get my dress on and zipped back up.

"I have a documentary to make," I remind him.

He scans me from top to toe and chuckles. "You look like you've been freshly fucked, Dakota. You're going to work like that?"

I roll my eyes. "Obviously I'm going to shower and change first."

"I can help you with both of those things," he offers, pulling me back down into the bed.

I laugh and let him wrap his arms around me and kiss the back of my neck, even while insisting, "I have work to do."

But still, I turn to face him full-on and brush his wild hair off his forehead, then capture his mouth with mine.

His hands slide down my thighs.

"Travis," I warn, gripping his wrists before this can go where I *really* would like it to.

He runs his tongue along my bottom lip. "Dakota."

My phone buzzes again.

"I have to go," I tell him firmly. "We need to see what usable footage we have. Apparently, the subject of our documentary absolutely hates interviews."

He stills. "What about the one we did?"

I don't react.

"You know. We were in Denver, and there was amazing pizza you kept stopping me from eating because you had so many questions."

"Of course I remember," I say evenly. "We're not going to use it."

"Dan doesn't want to?" Travis presses.

I exhale and prepare to confess. "I don't want to use it."

He eyes me curiously. "I told you that you could."

"I know," I say, shoving my feet into my shoes.

"Then why don't you?" Travis asks in a serious tone.

"Because you only said those things because it was *us*."

He cocks his head, taking in my expression, and I cut him off before he can open his mouth.

"Don't," I beg. "I'm having enough mental warfare about this whole situation already."

Travis reaches for his notebook, and I watch his fingers as he glides the pen over the page.

Mental warfare

I offer him a closed-mouth smile, then kiss him quickly before I lose my resolve.

When I've successfully returned to my own room, I'm almost disappointed to wash Travis off of me, but a shower and thorough hair-washing does wonders for my lingering headache and serves as a palate cleanser for my day ahead with Dan.

I pull on a fresh outfit, mindful of where Travis's stubble scratched the sensitive skin on my chest.

Part of me wants to delete the footage I have, just so it's not even a consideration to use in our documentary, but I can't bring myself to do that.

If I trace back through all our interactions, I can pinpoint that night of our personal interview as the one that sharply changed the trajectory of our relationship.

Selfishly, I want to keep it for myself.

I have to admit that he's not just an assignment to me anymore, and I don't think he has been for a while.

The revelation is pretty scary, not just because this is my *career* but because it's been mere weeks since we've become reacquainted, and I already feel strongly enough about him to withhold reporting.

And that makes me nauseated.

I frown as I enter Dan's hotel room that's been partially turned into an editing studio.

"You're late," he says by way of greeting.

I grab a bag of pretzels from his minibar. "You hungry? I want to order in."

"I think we have more important things to worry about," he says, gesturing to a few tabs of news articles he has open. "You're all over the news."

"Oh?" I ask on an exhale as I flip through the menu,

pretending this isn't life-changing information. "God, the gourmet grilled cheese sounds good."

"Dakota," Dan says sharply. "Look at this."

I relent and approach the desk, which has three monitors set up, along with his laptop.

As I expect, the screens display photos and videos of Travis and me, and I swoon just a tiny bit at how I look in his arms.

"Has Bryan seen this?" I ask tensely.

Dan shrugs. "No idea. The only reason I know about it is because Leigh showed me all the coverage on the gossip blogs over breakfast. She's already on it, though, doing damage control."

I do a quick scan of the articles, grateful that they're just gossip blogs who haven't even managed to track down my name yet.

That should buy me time to figure out how to handle this with Bryan and my own conscience—I honestly think it will have more complications for the latter.

But for now, I push off the attention.

"You had breakfast with Leigh?" I ask, raising an eyebrow.

He clears his throat and looks a little sheepish. "We do it almost every morning. She has been helping clarify, uh, scheduling and...yeah."

"Sure," I say knowingly, ribbing him despite the fact I have absolutely no ground to stand on. "So, how does she feel about the progress we've made so far?"

"She agrees that this documentary is nothing without Travis," Dan admits. "Hey, you wouldn't, by any chance, have taken some footage yesterday that we can use? Even just footage of him walking around?"

"Nothing usable," I tell him.

He sighs. "Well, then, let's just take a look at what we have."

"Not until I order my grilled cheese," I negotiate.

"Fine," he huffs.

After my room service has arrived and I'm sated, we spend the next eight hours combing through all the footage.

Dan has already done a momentous amount of work, cutting some of the best concert scenes from the numerous videos he has stored and stitching them together based on the original outline we worked on back in the New York offices.

So far, Leigh's interview serves as the base of the documentary, giving us the narrative from when she first met Travis and peppering it with little anecdotes of his growth over the past few years. Phoenix and Nick's accounts add some colorful commentary, as well as get into the weeds of recording and playing, balancing Leigh's somewhat positive spin on everything with grit and hard truths.

On a grading scale, I'd give the whole thing a C-.

We've got the basics, but there's nothing really spectacular or even interesting about the piece other than hearsay because we don't have the star's own voice in it.

Frankly, it's not publishable in its current state.

"We *need* Travis to sit down for an interview," Dan says firmly.

"I know," I admit.

Travis's personal voice would transform the entire

piece, filling in gaps about what truly makes him tick and sharing his own experiences of fame and performing on stage.

And yet, I understand why he's reluctant.

He has already given so much of himself to his career and to the public, I can't blame him for wanting to hold onto this last scrap of privacy.

He's contracted to do the tour and then he's done—so why would he pour his innermost self into this documentary that he's not even directly in control of?

Reflecting on that, I try to spin something that will make all parties involved happy.

"I had to take a feature-writing class in journalism school," I tell Dan.

He chuckles in surprise. "*You* took a feature class?"

I smile, sharing his amusement. "I did. Liberal arts school and all that. Anyway, we read some of the most famous profiles ever published, and my personal favorite was one on Frank Sinatra."

"Travis Young is no Frank Sinatra," Dan immediately argues. "Not even close."

"I'm not making that comparison. But the article is hailed as one of the best celebrity profiles ever written." I pause for emphasis. "And he didn't even talk to Sinatra. The whole piece is about how stressed out his staff was and how the people around him saw him, and it has influenced journalism and storytelling for decades."

"I see what you're trying to do with this. Look, Dakota, I know you're the award-winning writer and reporter here, and on paper, I'm just the guy with the camera. But I've done enough of these to know when there's a Travis

Young–sized hole in this documentary. We need him or our bosses are going to have our asses."

I chew on my bottom lip and toy with my phone, knowing I have the solution literally within my grasp.

But I still don't offer it up.

"Let's see what we can get after Vancouver," I suggest. "I want to take another look at the interview with Phoenix. I think there's more we can pull from it."

Dan's mouth presses into a thin line, but he doesn't argue.

So we spend the next day and a half nearly side by side, ordering in food and staring at the screens for so long, it feels like my eyes are bleeding.

TWENTY-ONE

Other than flying over a border and having to show off our passports when we land, our trip to Vancouver should feel like any other performance.

It *really* should.

But it doesn't.

Because of tension—the best kind, of course—between Travis and me.

It's like I'm tethered to him, even more fixated on his movements than I was before we had sex, and it's heightened even more by little secret touches.

Like how he chooses to sit beside me for the duration of the flight to Vancouver, listening to music on his headphones and staring out the window while he writes words on my thigh with his fingertip.

Or how his hand stays fixed on my lower back as he ushers me from the van to the hotel lobby.

But the truly devastating blow to normalcy is when Travis smiles at me when he sings as I stand offstage.

It seems like a simple gesture, really, and one that might be dismissed without a second thought by anyone else. But that little connection between us as he stands in front of a crowd of thousands of people, all screaming for him and singing along, guts me in a way that I never expected.

"Holy shit," I breathe.

Phoenix is too caught up in playing his instrument, thrashing his body to the beat, to notice, but Nick's eyes lock on mine, then he cocks his head toward Travis.

He's observant enough to see the shift in dynamic, but he's cool enough to simply smile and shrug as if it were some inevitable conclusion that doesn't warrant further reaction.

"Have you seen this?" Leigh says, coming up beside me and shoving her phone in my face.

I blink, taking in a splashy headline and photo of Travis carrying me, with a crowd of fans behind us.

"Yes," I admit. "Dan showed me the other day."

And ever since then, I've gotten a number of text messages and phone calls from a few friends and family members—including my *very* enthused mother—who want to press me for details, but I've brushed them off, saying the situation was misconstrued and I'm simply doing a story on him.

It's the same thing I told Bryan in a quick email this morning, and he has yet to reply.

"No," Leigh presses. "Scroll down."

I oblige her, skimming the article that's rife with specu-lation until one quote jars me enough that I gasp out loud.

"No fucking way," I murmur.

"Yes way," she hums.

"'Devin Young, Travis's brother and long-time manager, wouldn't speak on the record about the nature of the relationship between the musician and the *Exos* journalist.'" I stop and glance up at her. "Why is Devin talking to the press?"

"It gets worse," she promises, nodding back to the article.

"'He did imply over an email exchange that Travis has connections in every city—and whether that's for drugs, alcohol, gambling, or women, he didn't clarify when explicitly asked to—and simply said fans everywhere shouldn't let these photos deter them from getting their chance to party with Travis someday.'" I grind my teeth. "Great."

I've never seen Leigh look outright angry before, but she's clearly trying to hold it in. "Fucking idiot."

I hand the phone back to her and run my fingers through my hair.

Although the article won't derail things for him completely, this is not the type of opinion that necessarily *helps* a probation case. It will call Travis's judgment into question and further his bad reputation, which is just the sort of thing he doesn't need.

"What the hell was Devin thinking?" I ask.

Leigh huffs. "I don't think he ever does."

Travis quirks a brow at me, seeing the tension between Leigh and me even as he carries on singing the first encore song.

I plaster a smile on my face, trying to reassure him momentarily that everything is fine.

But when we're all gathered in the dressing room after the show, it all comes to a head.

Leigh keeps it together through the show, but now, with the crew preoccupied with dismantling the setup, she slams the door with our small group inside.

"What's wrong?" Travis asks, sidling up to me.

I don't have time to answer because Leigh's anger is palpable and steals everyone's attention. She's like a bull, dragging her feet on the carpet as she stomps over to Devin, who sits oblivious with a half-empty beer bottle in his fingertips.

"What the actual *fuck* is wrong with you?" she demands. "Tell me, Devin. I need to know what could possibly be going on in that pea-sized brain of yours, if you even have one at all."

Devin jumps in surprise at her proximity and rage, and his beer sloshes in the bottle, splashing a little bit on his jeans. "Aw, man, you made me spill."

Leigh winds up like she's going to smack the bottle out of his hand—or Devin himself—but clenches her fist at her side before she shoves her phone in his face.

"What were you even thinking?" she snaps. "Talking to a goddamn *tabloid* about your brother?"

"What?" Devin says innocently. "They reached out for a quote, wouldn't leave me alone. Practically harassed me, really, via email and social media, so I got rid of them."

"Who did what now?" Travis asks incredulously, leaving my side to approach the pair.

Leigh pinches the bridge of her nose as she hands over her phone.

I watch Travis skim through it and remain unfazed until he lands on the quote from his brother.

"'Fans everywhere shouldn't let these photos deter them from getting their chance to party with Travis someday,'" he reads in disbelief. "What the fuck is that supposed to mean?"

Devin shrugs. "Look, I thought it would be best to just deflect the situation. You know, give them a little bit to keep the fans engaged and hopeful."

"You think *this* is what engages my fans?" Travis argues.

"Well, it's certainly part of it. They buy into the whole Travis Young experience, the party-loving rockstar, not just the music."

Travis looks like his brother slapped him across the face.

"Even if that's true," Leigh snaps, "which it isn't, why would you think it's necessary, in any universe, for you to jump in?"

"If I kept ignoring their requests for comment, the speculation would just continue and get worse," Devin explains.

"I'm a *publicist*, Devin. I know how to handle this shit."

He ignores her and speaks directly to Travis. "Have you even seen all the photo manipulations and posts about the two of you?" he asks, then looks to me with wide eyes and raised hands like I'm somehow on his side.

But I let the professional handle it.

"Aside from the fact that you provided absolutely no information to diffuse the situation," Leigh says evenly, trying to find the composure she never fixed in place. "Have you forgotten that Travis is in the middle of a probationary period that hinges on maintaining a clean public persona?"

The venom in her voice stills even me.

"And now his own goddamn brother is quoted to be making him sound like some sort of irresponsible playboy, when all he has been doing for the past three years is focusing on his work!" Leigh shrieks at him.

I rub my temples and take in the rest of the room, noting that Nick and Phoenix are sitting close together, watching the scene unfold with stunned expressions.

My stomach drops when my gaze lands on Dan, who is documenting every single second of this exchange with his brow furrowed.

He looks at me, seeming perplexed by the conversation, but as he takes in my lack of surprise, his expression changes to one of irritation—likely at my clear withholding of information on Travis's legal troubles—and shakes his head.

"I'm sorry," Devin says finally, and he has the good sense to look sheepish. "I wasn't thinking."

"Clearly," Leigh breathes.

Devin drains the rest of his beer and sets the bottle on the table before he cracks open another, not even bothering to toss the empty one into the bin that's a foot away.

I watch Travis meet Leigh's gaze in silent conversation.

After a moment, he shoves his hands in his pockets and directs his full attention to his brother. "Devin, I hate to be the one who says this, but it's probably time you went home," he says, not totally unkindly.

His brother snorts and takes a sip of his beer. "Funny, man."

Travis's jaw ticks. "I'm serious. I've already stripped down the tour to the most minimum staff to keep the drama out and focus on work. And you're making it difficult. I'll get you a flight back to Pittsburgh tomorrow morning if you want, but you're not coming along with us for the rest of the tour."

"You're fucking kidding me, right?" Devin scoffs, flicking his gaze around the room.

I'm the only one, aside from Travis, who meets his eyes.

"You're sending your own brother packing just because of one little quote in some piece-of-shit gossip publication?" Devin demands, nervously running a hand through his hair. "All for some journalist who can't keep it in her pants long enough to get an interview from you?"

Travis's fist clenches at his side, and I reach out, putting a hand on his arm before the verbal sparring turns to physical blows.

"It's fine," I tell Travis, trying to reassure him.

I've already seen Travis throw a punch to defend a stranger's honor, and even though Devin's an asshole, I refuse to drive an even bigger wedge between them.

"The party's been over for a long time, Devin," Travis says sharply. "Everyone sees it but you."

Devin's expression is helpless at first, then I see the anger tick up, and, finally, the disbelief. "You know what? I've been with you your whole career, dude. Making sure you're happy and drugged up, or clean, or whatever the fuck you want to do in whatever city with whoever, and I'm done. No more ride-or-die from me. Fuck this shit. I'm out of here."

He winds up and throws his beer at the wall, sending foaming liquid and sharp shards of glass everywhere.

I jump back to avoid the ricochet, and Travis catches me in his arms.

Devin, with one final shake of his head, leaves us all in stunned silence.

TWENTY-TWO

Bryan calls me when we're on the flight to Chicago, but I don't pick up.

For one, I actually don't know if I'm allowed to talk on the phone while on a private flight, and also, I just don't feel like talking to him.

It might be a little insubordinate to ignore my boss, but I don't really have it in me to care at this moment because I'm too off-put by the turn of events.

The mood on the plane is oddly somber.

Even Travis has retreated into his own mind, alternating between chewing his thumbnail and jotting things down in his notebook.

I reach for him under the table and squeeze his thigh in reassurance, earning a genuine smile, even if there's a little sadness in his eyes.

"You okay?" I ask him quietly.

"It was probably overdue," he admits. "But it still sucks."

I nod. "Yeah. It does."

"Will you stay with me tonight?" he asks, brushing a lock of hair away from my face.

"Yes," I say without hesitation.

Travis bites his lip to stop himself from smiling fully, then turns his attention back to his notebook.

When I open my computer, a notification pops up in my inbox, and I frown at the sight of a new message from Bryan, titled "STOP IGNORING ME AND READ THIS."

I open it immediately.

Dakota,

This is your boss. Bryan. Remember me? Haven't heard from you in a while, but Dan has been keeping me updated on your progress. I like the clips I'm seeing, especially the interview with the publicist. Eager to see what else you've got.

There's progress on the Ellison case. The legal team is confident that it's time to start reporting again. I'm sure you've seen Christina's follow-up, which has gotten some nice pickup, but we've recently got a tip on our general line, and it needs your attention. Possibly enough for you to fly back to New York.

I should have more information for you when you land in Chicago, but for Christ's sake, answer your boss when he calls.

Bryan

I clench my jaw after I've read through his email for the third time, trying to decide what I like less—the attitude in his tone, the news of Christina's follow-up, or Bryan's vagueness on what he has for me.

My fingers fly across the keyboard.

Bryan,

What is the tip?

Dakota

I imagine him rolling his eyes at my directness, but I don't have much patience for pleasantries.

I refresh my inbox every three minutes until the plane is somewhere over Minnesota, when his response finally comes through.

Dakota,

So nice to hear from you. Ellison's estranged daughter has been calling the general line here every day trying to get ahold of you. I happened to pick up, got her talking, and discovered exactly who she was.

I need you to fly out first thing in the morning. I will arrange your ticket. Come directly to the newsroom from the airport, and I'll give you the full rundown on what we've dug up so far. She wants to meet tomorrow—and given how flighty she seems, this might be our only shot. She'll only talk to you.

Bryan

The strangeness of this arrangement isn't lost on me, but I once had a source who only wanted to meet in the middle of the night at an empty diner for fear she was being followed, so I suppose it's not that far-fetched.

But it's only as Travis's leg nudges mine, in a totally innocent and unintentional move, that I realize what I'm giving up if I fly back to New York.

Bryan,

What about the Travis story?

Dakota

My fingers shake slightly as they hover over the keyboard.

Dakota,

Don't tell me you've come around to it?

Bryan

I rub my temples.

Bryan,

I'll see you tomorrow.

Dakota

I close my laptop and don't mention a word of it to Travis or anyone else as I try to process how this can play out.

We've just started whatever this is, and it's all very complicated.

Say I fly back to New York, diving right back into where I left off and want to pick back up on the Ellison story, then what?

I finish the documentary?

Or Dan finishes it?

Then Travis leaves for more touring and then...

I don't even know how that will work or what my ideal situation is or what I really even want at this point.

And that indecision is absolutely terrifying for someone like me.

I'm distracted enough by my thoughts to not be nervous about the plane landing and happily let Travis guide me through the motions of arriving and getting settled into our hotel. I don't even bother with the pretense of heading to my own room, letting the bellhop take both of our suitcases directly up to Travis's suite.

When we're alone, I kick off my shoes and collapse on the couch. "I need a drink."

He opens the fridge and frowns. "Not much of a selection in this one."

"Is that a little thing of vodka?" I ask.

"I thought you were a tequila fan?"

"Right now, I'm a fan of anything that will take the edge off."

He lets the door shut and stands up, stalking over to me. "Dakota, you don't need alcohol for that."

"I don't?" I ask innocently.

Travis drops to his knees and runs his hands up my legs, thumbing the edge of my skirt as he looks up at me.

"No," he answers. "You don't."

My instinct is to close my eyes and relax into the way his mouth moves up my thigh, but I force my gaze to stay fixed on him, needing to see this for myself.

Travis doesn't bother removing any of my clothes. He forces my skirt up over my thighs and bunches it at my waist, then smirks before pulling down my lace panties and tossing them over his shoulder.

His hands grip my thighs just a second before he laps me up in long strokes, up and down. His movement is almost lazy, like he's content to do this for hours on end, but it makes me squirm with further need.

"Travis," I groan.

"Relax," he murmurs. "I'm taking the edge off."

My head hits the back of the couch as his tongue taps my clit in a pulsating rhythm, and I jut my hips forward, getting off not only by the feeling of his tongue but by how fucking unbelievably sexy he looks.

He keeps up the motion as he slides one finger, then two, inside me, hitting that spot that makes my toes curl.

I'm not even undressed, but soon, I'm completely undone, struggling to keep my eyes open as my inner walls contract around his fingers.

Everything feels so fucking good, and we've barely gotten started.

He stands in a single, fluid motion and unbuckles his belt with urgency, shoving down his pants and boxer briefs just enough to let his cock spring free.

I moan at the sight, and Travis pulls me upright, bringing my lips to his in a bruising kiss before he spins me around.

Gripping the back of the couch as my knees hit the cushion, I pant in anticipation at him taking me from this angle.

He slides a condom on, and then, without further warning, he surges into me.

"Fuck," we cry out in unison.

Even though I'm still coming down from my first orgasm, I feel the waves of the second one building as his hips snap against mine.

His hands roam over my ass cheeks and grip my hips as the wet smacking sounds increase in volume the longer he continues his punishing pace.

And all I can do is grip the furniture and hold myself upright as I go along for the ride.

I turn to look at him over my shoulder, and when our eyes lock, he grins.

"You feeling it yet?" he pants.

I'm unable to form thoughts other than his name and swear words, so I nod.

He reaches around to my front, catching my swollen clit with his long fingers. "How about now?"

"Travis," I moan as my knees buckle.

He climbs up on the couch behind me, anchoring his knees between mine as a support. Travis pulls me to his chest, somehow still surging inside me, and licks the side of my neck.

"I want another one," he purrs. "Are you close?"

"Y-yes," I manage to say.

229

"Good. Because I'm ready to go inside you and fill you up with everything I have."

Those words, combined with the way he pinches my clit, send me over the edge, and he falls along with me.

TWENTY-THREE

I should have told Travis last night.

It wasn't that I didn't have the opportunity to—I could have told him on the plane when I found out or on the car ride from the airport or getting fucked on the couch and the shower.

But I didn't.

I let myself push it off and just live in the moment with him, ignoring the call back to reality and plenty of difficulty for just a little longer.

And now, freshly clean, fully dressed, and completely packed before he's even awake, I realize my mistake.

"Hey," he says, sitting up and rubbing his eyes. "Where are you off to?"

It's a repeat of the last time we did this, but instead of only running down the hall, I'm flying halfway across the country with no idea if I'll return or when I'll see him next.

"New York."

He blinks. "Are you serious?"

"Yes," I admit solemnly. "I have to go back for the Ellison story. There's a new lead, and she'll only speak to me, apparently."

"Today?"

"Right now. My car's almost here."

He stands up and slides on his jeans from yesterday, and I have to force myself not to appreciate how low they are on his hips.

"How long will you be gone for?" Travis asks.

"I'm not sure."

His eyes narrow. "But what about the rest of the tour?"

"I asked my boss about that yesterday, and he said we'd—"

"You knew about this *yesterday*, and I'm just hearing about it now?" Travis says in disbelief.

"I know," I tell him. "I just...I'm sorry. With everything that blew up with Devin, I just didn't want to add to it, and then we were enjoying ourselves. And now I have to catch this flight."

"Don't let what he said freak you out," he pleads. "Despite what my idiot brother says, I'm not just some rockstar who runs around, getting high and wasted and hooking up with anyone at all."

He pauses and runs a hand through his hair.

"Anymore," he adds.

"It's not that," I promise him. "I mean, not fully. But I just wasn't expecting all of this, and now I'm defaulting back to what I know and I'm..."

Travis pulls me into his arms. "Scared and wondering if it's worth it."

My phone pings to signal the car is waiting for me downstairs, and I pull back.

"Dakota, I don't have all the answers or right goddamn words at this exact moment, but I just know that I don't want this to end. Not until we've figured out if it's something."

"You're about to go off around the world, traveling and touring, and that's not my life, Travis," I say sadly, hating myself just a little for imagining it could be. "This story... I've been chasing it for a year. I *have* to go back. It's my job. My *life* is on pause right now."

"Right," he says, devoid of any emotion that causes me to bristle. "And this was just some temporary thing."

I wince as I grab my purse and the handle on my suitcase. "You, of all people, should understand the desire to further a career."

He doesn't respond for a moment.

"All for the story, then?" Travis says lifelessly.

"Of course not," I flinch, ignoring the reminder notification from my phone that my driver is waiting. "I don't have a choice here."

"Of course you have a choice," Travis argues, a little desperately.

"So you want me to give up on a story that I've spent a year of my life on, only to stand around and watch you, and do more to promote *your* career?" I lash back.

He shakes his head and lowers his volume. "I'd never ask you to do any of that. I'm just asking for a little clarity, and maybe a little give and take from your end."

I get a notification that I have three minutes to get down before the car leaves, and my heart pounds from the pressure of both wanting to leave and hating myself for doing this.

"Travis," I sigh, stepping up to press a quick peck on his lips. "This doesn't have to be a big dramatic conversation or fight or moment where things spill out and get all messy. We've only spent a few weeks together, but we're both mature adults now, who have the reality of a story to do and a tour to complete. We can just...let things go."

"Let things go," he repeats.

"Yeah," I say, urging him to relent.

"You know, I've taken you for many things, Dakota, but cruel isn't one of them."

"I'm not trying to be," I promise. "I'm just being honest."

"Cold, hard facts, then?" Travis says.

"Always."

His expression hardens. "Then let me tell you something, Dakota. The truth? You're scared."

I balk at that. "This decision has nothing to do with you, Travis."

"No," Travis insists, crossing his arms on his chest. "You going back to New York is logical, but you not wanting to tell me until the last possible second...*that* is a coward's move."

My anger overtakes my sadness, but he doesn't give me a chance to let it out.

"You're not afraid to dig into everyone else's lives, but you're not used to opening yourself up," he continues. "I didn't really understand it at first, chalking the deflections and observations up to being a reporter, but at every instance, you push the attention, the focus, on to everyone else. And let me tell you, Dakota, I see you, and I *like* what I see. Every single inch of you. I'm just asking you not to shut me out and lose yourself...and me."

I open and close my mouth a few times, stunned by his declaration, as a final notification hits for me to get in the car before I lose it.

"I'm sorry, Travis," I tell him as I renew my grip on my belongings and walk away. "I just *really* can't do all this right now."

This situation is totally unfair, and it's not lost on me that this is the second relationship in a row—if that term even applies here—where I've left things in flux. It didn't work out so well with Mark, but I can't recall ever feeling as gutted as I do now.

I've adjusted to this routine of living in the moment, watching performances, stressing about interviews, flying around, and enjoying Travis. And I've let it get to me more than I should have, making his life my own.

The ambiguity, though, is a bit of a bitch.

I'm definitely going to want closure one way or another, but I think we both need time and a little distance to resurface and move forward. I could open my phone and call him or send him a text with an apology, but somehow, that seems like a cop-out.

He deserves better than an after-the-fact conversation over the phone, and I still *have* to leave. Because even though I want to turn around and jump back in bed and on tour with Travis, I have a job to do.

That's what I try to focus on, distracting myself from

the takeoff, bumpy plane ride, and rocky landing by rereading my notes and interviews on the Ellison case for the hundredth time. I even read Christina's follow-up story, which is basically just a regurgitation of my original story with updated "no comment" quotes from Ellison Incorporated executives and government officials.

I try not to let my bitterness fester as I make my way through the airport, then catch the train and consider the opportunities this new lead may present me.

By the time I get to the *Exos* building, I move with determination.

I've already done the hard part of leaving Travis. I need to make this worth it and do what I came here to do before I figure out all the rest.

I unlock the door to the newsroom because even though I've flown halfway across the country, I'm still the first one in the office.

It feels strange to take a seat in my chair—something that was a welcome part of my daily routine before but now feels almost foreign.

"Dakota!" Christina squeals excitedly.

I turn to see her and Bryan walking into the newsroom, noting that my boss looks exhausted, even though it's not yet ten o'clock.

"You're back!" Christina declares.

I smile at her. "I am."

"I've seen the articles," she gushes. "I mean, people are speculating about you and him. And the pictures of the two of you together! Imagine when they find out it's just because you're doing a documentary and not, like, living everyone's dream life. But, ugh. You must have incredible coverage."

"So far so good," I say nonchalantly.

"I need details, Dakota! What's it like to be backstage? Are his bandmates cool? Is he even sexier in person? That picture—"

Bryan clears his throat. "Dakota," he says, beckoning me into his office with a tilt of his head.

"Sorry," I say to Christina, even though I'm not all that sorry.

"We'll have to catch up later," she says.

"Sure." My tone is dismissive but not totally unkind. "Saw your article, by the way."

Her face falters slightly. "Oh, okay," she stammers.

I don't mean to make her nervous, but I can't hide my annoyance.

Still, I remember what it felt like to see my name on a published piece for the first time.

"Congrats on your first byline," I tell her as I reach Bryan's door. "One of many, I'm certain."

She brightens at that. "Thank you," she says sincerely.

The pile of wrappers and cans on Bryan's desk is the biggest I've seen in recent memory, and that doesn't exactly give me feelings of reassurance.

"So, what's the deal?" I ask, cutting directly to it. "When am I meeting the daughter?"

He checks his watch. "In about ten minutes."

"Ten minutes?" I nearly shriek as I stand. "What the hell, Bryan? Why do you keep throwing this last-minute shit on me? What if I missed my flight or couldn't get a cab or something?"

"We would have dealt with it," Bryan says with a shrug, brushing me off.

"And where am I meeting her?" I ask.

"In the alley behind the building. She's going to show up in an inconspicuous gray sedan at approximately 10:12, and you're going to hop in."

"And go where?" I ask.

"I'm not sure."

I roll my eyes. "This seems like a great way to get kidnapped. Or worse."

Bryan chuckles. "Look, if you're really not comfortable with it, we can figure something else out."

"I'm already out the door," I say, grabbing my phone.

Though I often deal with criminals for my job, exposing their wrongdoings and harmful behaviors, I've never once truly felt unsafe.

Probably because I'm mostly hidden at my desk and behind a computer, doing research or conducting phone interviews. Although, I occasionally meet people in person to gather quotes and have attended court proceedings a number of times.

But today, even as I idle near a dumpster and watch people go about their daily lives on the other side of the street, I still feel a little exposed.

I hold myself as confidently as I can in my heels and smart dress, but when the described car pulls up right on time, my hands shake as I open the door and slide into the passenger's side.

"Dakota Shaw," the woman in the driver's seat says evenly.

"Jacqueline Ellison," I return the greeting.

Even if I hadn't seen several pictures of her over the years, I'd recognize the resemblance to her scumbag father, despite the red wig, sunglasses, and nose jobs I'm willing to bet she's had.

She glances around, ensuring there's no one nearby, though I'm not sure who or what is making her so paranoid.

"My boss said that you want to talk?" I pull up my voice recorder app. "Is it okay if I record this?"

"No," she says forcefully. "I'm not talking on the record."

I quirk a brow at her. "Then why am I here?"

She takes another look around, twitching slightly as she does.

I chew on the inside of my cheek and wonder if this is a gigantic waste of time, and that impression is not alleviated when she puts her hand down the front of her shirt.

"Here." After digging around in her bra, she holds out a flash drive.

I tentatively take it, a little skeeved out by how warm it is. "What's on this?"

"Financial records of Ellison Incorporated for the past ten years, along with statements from offshore accounts, and as much data as I could scrape from my father's personal laptop."

Suddenly, the little flash drive doesn't seem too repulsive to grip in my fingertips.

"How did you get these?" I ask skeptically.

"My father's laptop password is my first name," she mumbles. "But some of these accounts are in my name to deflect attention from him because he was stupid enough to think I would go along with that quietly, so I have access to a lot of the information."

"You sure you don't want to give this to the feds?"

"I cooperated with them years ago, and nothing ever came of it. I'm pretty sure my father bought and paid for his innocence, but he discovered my part in his exposure in the process, so he's cut me off financially."

"So you're motivated to take him down," I conclude.

"I didn't think it was possible until your article came out. Let's just say you've accomplished more with that one piece than any government agency has in twenty years."

I want to smile, but I know that won't go over well at the moment. "And you're sure you don't want to speak on the record?"

She shakes her head. "I need to disappear for a while. I'm sure once you publish, people will come looking for me."

For the first time I really and truly consider the danger that sources put themselves in.

I'd be lying if I said it hasn't occurred to me before, but my sources are usually anonymous, unidentifiable by their vague details and job titles, or low enough in the company that no one would want to bother with them, even if their names were in print.

But it's because of Travis that I have this new under-standing, this empathy for people who speak out, and even more for Jacqueline, who took a big risk in getting me this information.

"I should go," Jacqueline says.

"Right," I say, shifting closer to the door. "I don't

suppose there's a way for me to contact you if I have questions?"

She smiles, but her attempt at being reassuring is almost pathetic. "You won't have questions. I promise you that."

TWENTY-FOUR

It takes me two weeks to get through all the files from Jacqueline.

I sort through them on an old laptop that's not connected to the internet or anything *Exos*-related, just to be safe, and the only time the computer is out of my sight is when I'm showering.

Even though I make backup copies of everything, I'm terrified I'm going to lose the treasure trove of information she gave me.

Bryan and I have to pull in our legal team for every step of my reporting process to pinpoint which documents are most likely to get us sued, but the department is actually eager to have more ammunition to get the libel trial dismissed.

It takes another week for *Exos* to hire a firm who specializes in this kind of financial information, then another to finish writing the piece.

I drown myself in the numbers and words and information, and it distracts me from missing Travis. Because I find that even though we're apart, he's still a part of my routine.

I catch myself humming the chorus to "Vantage Point" as I shampoo my hair. I stop myself from wondering what he's up to, recalling what city he's likely in at this point, thinking of him as I slide on the dress I wore to the meeting with the record executives. I catch myself jotting down one-liners that I overhear. I get a midday sugar crash and frown at the lack of lollipops available at the bodega around the corner.

It's at night, though, just before I fall asleep and catch the near-midnight hour on my phone that I feel the ache the most. I always promise myself as I'm slipping away into dreams that tomorrow will be the day I apologize to him, but in the cold light of day the next morning, the ache has dissipated just enough to remind myself that he hasn't reached out to me either.

By the time I hit publish on the story—one of my fastest turnarounds to-date, given the level of legal red tape and the amount of information presented—it's been more than a month since I left him in that hotel room.

And nothing reminds me of that more viscerally than when I bump into Dan in the hallway.

"Dan?" I say, somewhat bewildered. "You're back already?"

"Bryan didn't tell you?"

Dread rolls over me. "Tell me what?"

"The record label asked if we'd be able to time the publication of our documentary with the start of the European tour. Apparently, they're talking about doing some sort of special release with a little red carpet and everything."

"So we work for the label now?" I ask icily.

Dan shrugs. "I'm just doing what I'm told."

"And what is that, exactly?"

"Well, I'm just about to show Bryan a rough cut of some things I've filmed," he says tentatively.

"Good. I'll come with you."

He sighs and waves for me to follow him.

Bryan is already in the editing room when we arrive, sipping his third Diet Coke of the day. "Dakota, are you joining us?"

"The Ellison story went live this morning," I remind him, as if he doesn't know. "So I assume I'm back on the Travis Young story?"

"Why don't you show off what you two have put together," Bryan suggests, ignoring my direct question.

Dan smiles tightly at me before he presses play.

It's not all that different from the last iteration of the compilation Dan and I went through; although, he's put in a few more clips and songs from cities I missed with my premature return to New York.

He also got an off-the-cuff comment from Phoenix about how alive he feels when performing, supercut over him standing at the front of the stage and pounding on his chest, which makes Bryan chuckle.

And there's a five-minute addition of Nick and Phoenix talking about how meticulous Travis is, supported by clips from soundchecks and footage of Travis strumming his guitar on the plane.

But when Travis himself appears on the screen, walking

into a room I don't recognize and sitting down for what appears to be a true interview, I brace myself.

Dan plays both videographer and interviewer, and it's a little tough to watch because of how disjointed the questions are, but Leigh chimes in from off-camera to fill in the gaps, prompting Travis to redeliver some of his responses.

"This is unethical," I say, purely out of idealistic habit. "You're having a publicist feed lines to an interview subject."

Both Dan and Bryan ignore me, continuing to watch as Travis delivers only two complete and usable soundbites.

The rest of the project is just how I left it.

As the screen goes blank, I breathe a sigh of relief, glad it's over and there's nothing incriminating about Travis, myself, or both of us together. But I don't relax too much because I'm also aware of how much Bryan is going to hate this.

He polishes off the rest of his Diet Coke, then says exactly what I expect. "There's no grit to this. Nothing to the story other than Travis being a stickler for playing on time and in tune, along with some anecdotes about their happy times together."

"You once told me that we could just stitch together an hour of Travis shirtless and it'd be good to go," I retort.

"And obviously I meant that," he says sarcastically. "We need more meat to this, and we're almost out of time."

"Well," Dan interjects. "I do have a few clips we could add."

I grind my molars together.

"Play them," Bryan orders, waving his hand toward the computer.

Dan cues up what he has to offer, and as he presses play, a sickening feeling hits my stomach.

They're rough cuts, stitched together, and the jarring start-and-stop to the clips is almost as bad as the content.

The first batch is Devin in various scenarios, making crude gestures to the camera or chatting up women. I can't help but be amused at the supercut of him stumbling around with a beer in his hand, but I barely conceal my shock as it fades into him doing a line of cocaine backstage, only to stand up and throw his arms around Travis in excitement, then begin the pre-show pump-up ritual.

To the untrained eye, it looks like Travis is condoning this behavior, but Dan and I both know the truth—he would have gotten rid of his brother a long time ago if he knew he was carrying that shit around.

The next clips cast an unflattering light on Travis.

On screen, he yells at Nick in frustration after a particularly grueling day of travel followed by a mediocre performance, then the viewpoint shifts, and he's jumping down into the crowd to punch the guy who tried to grope that innocent girl, then, finally, he's basically telling that interviewer in Seattle to fuck off.

But the shit show isn't over yet.

The last clip is, surprisingly, of Nick and Phoenix. I recognize their outfits and hairstyles and realize this is from the first night I was backstage with them.

What stands out in my mind about that night is that it was the first real conversation Travis and I had—but then I immediately recall what kept us enclosed in the green room together.

"Oh no," I mumble.

Although the camera is a little shaky, Dan picks up the tail end of their argument, then catches Phoenix's attempt to console Nick. At first, Nick pushes him off, but whatever Phoenix says gets him to let his guard down enough to fall into the other man's embrace. They share a passionate kiss before breaking apart and renewing their fight once again.

The clip stops as the camera lowers.

Judging by the look I'm seeing on Dan's face right now, he wishes he never caught it.

"We can't use any of those," I say immediately.

Bryan laughs in delight. "Like hell we can't. *These* are what will make the story."

"This isn't even an accurate portrayal of who these people are," I argue. "It's just feeding gossip and making them all look like unhinged rockstars."

"That's up for our readers and viewers to decide," Bryan pushes back. "It's your job to report and frame the narrative."

"But everyone will just sensationalize it."

"Which is even better for us," Bryan says.

I shake my head. "This is unethical."

"This is exposure of the behind-the-scenes life of Travis Young. It gives more insight into who he is."

"Please tell me how outing the fucked-up relationship between his two bandmates has anything to do with who Travis Young is," I bite out.

Bryan rubs the back of his neck. "You knew, then?"

"Of course I knew," I snap. "I'm your *best reporter*, Bryan."

Dan fidgets nervously, then clears his throat. "Travis

mentioned something about an interview you and he did one night in Denver?"

I know he's trying to offer up an alternative to defuse the tension, but it makes everything worse.

"You built a personal relationship enough with our subject to have the tabloids accuse you of *dating*, and now I'm hearing you have a private interview with him that's not included in here?" Bryan roars. "Are you kidding me?"

It's not that I falter at my boss's accusatory tone, but it forces me to make a decision on the fly—I am not willing to compromise about this.

This isn't just some story of someone else's life that I can walk away from once it's on the website.

This is Travis's life.

And mine.

And, hopefully, our life together—if he's still game for it.

Given what I'm about to do, I sure as hell hope I haven't missed my chance.

"I can't be a part of this," I say forcefully.

Bryan rolls his eyes. "The door's right there, Dakota. I'm not going to placate you about this project or direction any longer. If you don't want to do it, then don't."

I shake my head. "No. Not just this story or argument or single day."

His look of complete disbelief is enough of an affirmation that my decision is the right one.

Because in all the years of coaching, friendship, and late nights, this is the moment Bryan—and I—realizes that while I'm eager to grow and challenge myself, I'm not totally malleable to the *Exos* machine.

While I have appreciated the career growth and support for some of my more controversial stories from both him and the company, it's taken me until this moment, right here, to draw the firm line.

I've spent too much time worried about the ethics of reporting that I haven't faced my own personal code of morality head on. I won't expose him just for the sake of my company's whims and shock value, even if it will benefit me in the end.

Travis Young is not a topic or person I'm going to bend for any longer—I'm going to completely break them.

"I'm done here, Bryan," I say simply.

"You're shitting me, right?"

I shake my head. "I'm dead serious. I'm walking."

"That means no credit," he reminds me. "No big bonus check or producer title or anything at all. You leave now, and you're done with nothing to show for it."

I already earmarked a big chunk of that for my credit card bill, so it's a little bit of a gut punch, but I stand strong as he continues.

"You just published a story that's going to shoot your name to the top of every single award ballot for the next year, and you just want to spit on everything we've done here?"

He's angry.

I get it because I am too—at him, myself, this situation.

But there are some things I'm not going to stand for. This position of hurting good people for clicks is one of them, no matter how much history Bryan and I have.

"Thank you for everything, Bryan," I say calmly before I leave the room.

I don't look back, my eyes set dead ahead as I move to my desk and ignore the congratulations I get from random people while I grab my belongings.

"Dakota, wait!"

Dan calls after me as I make my way down the hall toward the exit.

"Nothing you say is going to change my mind," I tell him, slowing my pace slightly. "I'm done here."

"I figured," he admits, catching up to me. "But you should hold onto this."

He presses a flash drive into my palm.

"These clips don't exist anywhere else. Don't get me wrong, I'm not about to bail on my job, but...that doesn't mean I think anyone else deserves to see this."

"Thank you," I tell him as I grip it in my hand.

He nods. "I don't know if you've thought of this, but tonight's their final show in the U.S. before they head out to Europe..."

I blink, recalling their tour poster in my mind. "In Pittsburgh."

"And I'm sure Leigh would arrange a pass for you, if you wanted one," he says lightly.

"Thanks, Dan. For everything."

I turn away and walk out of *Exos* with my curiosity burning and absolutely no regrets.

TWENTY-FIVE

I buy my plane ticket while I'm on the train back to my apartment.

And for someone who doesn't like flying, I've really been pushing the limit lately.

Once I'm through my door, I barely have time to shove clothes into a bag before I have to leave and hail a cab. I'm ridiculously lucky that there's no traffic as we speed toward LaGuardia, but I'm cutting it close.

Even though I breeze through security upon my arrival, I am the last person to board the plane.

The only seat I could get was in the back, so I swallow down my rising fear as I make my way past all the other passengers, who are just as impatient as I am to be on the way.

I don't have any of my coping mechanisms in place as we take off—no Travis, no work to distract me, no Tootsie Pops present—so I just hold onto the resolve that as soon as we pass the required altitude, I'll finally be able to pull out my laptop and watch whatever Dan wanted to hide from the world.

When the bell chimes overhead and the flight attendant announces the use of approved electronic devices, I'm practically bouncing as I grab my laptop and headphones.

The woman next to me doesn't seem enthused by my erratic movements, but I don't give a shit, turning my computer so the window and I are the only viewers.

It's almost a relief when Travis's face comes on my screen.

He's sitting for the same interview that Dan apparently conducted in my absence, but this clip is just as he's getting mic'd up.

"Have you heard from her?" Travis asks, unable to mask the sadness in his tone.

My heart flutters.

"No, I haven't," Dan says.

Travis nods. "Do you know if she's coming back?"

"I'm not...I don't think so, Travis. She got some massive break with her Ellison story. My colleagues are mad because she and her editor are being all secretive with what she has, but it's going to be *huge* from what I can tell."

"Good for her," Travis says genuinely. "Do you think—"

"Travis," Leigh chides. "Focus on the interview."

Then the video cuts, but the screen doesn't go blank.

For the next two minutes, I'm treated to a supercut of little interactions between Travis and me. The moments are quick and short, but it feels like someone is squeezing my heart as I take in each one.

I see pure adoration on Travis's face as he watches me

focus on my phone, but he pulls his expression neutral as I happen to glance up at him.

There are a few moments like that, when he's staring at an oblivious me, and then we start to get more comfortable around each other, until eventually, after that fateful day in Seattle, we graduate to the little touches between us I thought no one else saw.

Travis apparently goes into full protector mode every time we're out in public. That hand I felt on my back isn't purely for the benefit of him touching me—he's scoping out our surroundings to make sure the mob isn't going to swallow us as we move.

He always has eyes on me, according to the camera, and makes sure I'm taken care of, seated in the van or settled in for lunch, before he relaxes.

It's odd to see a replay of my life this way, and I'm sure there's so much I've missed while so singularly focused on my own problems, career, and wants.

I've been so short-sighted from the moment I got this assignment, and I'm a little ashamed of myself for it.

Travis, to his credit or his insanity, managed to see past it all, eventually trusting and opening up to me, even with our uncertain future and everything he had to lose.

In the end, though, I'm the one who has arguably lost the most—at least where my identity and my job are concerned—and I'm oddly at peace with it.

I spend the rest of the flight checking my phone every five seconds, mentally urging the pilot forward and running every possible calculation of traffic and routes to ensure I get to the show in time.

When we land, I sprint to the rental car counter as I

shoot off a text to Leigh, then fidget until she confirms there's a pass waiting for me at will call.

I make it to the concert midway through their set, and even though I've never been to this particular venue before, it feels like coming home.

There's something about being back in Travis's and my childhood town and taking in the familiar skyline that makes me appreciate our past in a way that's going to help us form our future together—if he still wants one.

Leigh gives me a hug when I arrive backstage, and a few of the crew members smile and wave without interrupting the flow of managing what's happening with the show.

I take a minute to change into a less formal outfit in the dressing room, which thankfully didn't get too wrinkled in my bag, then touch up my makeup in the mirror before I go stand in the wings.

Nick notices me first, doing a double take as he leads the guys through the second verse of "Same Conclusions, But We're Different."

He yells up to Phoenix, who waves at me with his drumstick, then they go back to rocking out—as they should—vibing off the incredible energy of the hometown crowd.

Meanwhile, Travis closes his eyes as he belts out the lyrics, opening them again when he turns to witness Phoenix's drum solo, only for his gaze to get caught up with mine.

He blinks, seemingly not trusting his own vision at first, then grins.

I swear his eyes don't turn back to the audience until the band finishes their main set and breaks before the encore, and then he dashes off the stage to scoop me up into his arms.

The force of his mouth on mine is overpowering, and I give him everything I have, locking my legs around his waist and squealing in delight as he pulls me even closer.

He steps back from our momentum, edging onto the stage enough that people from a certain angle can see us making out, and they scream his name and cheer even louder.

I break the kiss and laugh, but Travis ignores the crowd.

"What does this mean?" he asks, lowering me back to the floor. "You're back on the project?"

I laugh. "No."

"Then what are you doing here?" Travis asks.

"Well, I kind of quit my job."

He balks. "What?"

"And I'm here to see you."

The crowd noise is almost deafening, but I know Travis has no intention of returning to the stage until he has my explanation, so I blurt the words out quickly.

"*Exos* is planning on turning your documentary into a sensationalized piece of garbage."

"I'll take care of it," Leigh promises us, coming out of nowhere, then she looks a little sheepish. "Sorry for eavesdropping, but you could have picked a more private place for that conversation."

I brush past her apology. "How are you possibly going to fix this?"

"In the contract, the label has first dibs on outright buying the footage instead of letting *Exos* publish it as a documentary."

"Good," I say, relieved. "Well, for us, but kind of shitty I gave so many years of my life to a place with those types of practices."

"The label will be okay with this?" Travis clarifies.

Leigh shrugs. "I'll splice some of the footage into a little promo for social media, so it won't be a total waste."

Travis drops a kiss on the top of my head. "I wouldn't call it a waste anyway."

I grin as his arms tighten around me.

Nick clears his throat as he steps up to us. "Sorry, but, uh, we should probably finish the show, yeah?"

"Yes," Travis agrees eagerly, catching my mouth once more before the three of them jog back out.

Maybe it's just the high I feel right now that's making me a little biased, but the three-song encore set that follows is the best performance I've seen so far.

TWENTY-SIX

"Yes, Mom," I say into my phone.

"And you'll both come for dinner tonight?" she asks me for the fifth time.

"Yes, Mom," I repeat, patience wearing thin.

She huffs. "A little heads-up would have been nice."

"If you're not ready for us, we'll just go straight to London," I tease.

"I'll see you at seven," she says firmly. "Bring wine. And tequila."

I laugh. "Okay. See you then."

"Love you, Dakota."

"Love you, too."

I hang up and smile, allowing myself to feel light and happy.

But then I take in the dreary brown painted wall of the courthouse, too aware of the coin toss that's happening right behind the closed double doors.

It's not that I'm nervous about the outcome of Travis's

hearing, but if I'm being honest, having my boyfriend walk out of his own volition and not be escorted away in handcuffs is very much my preferred outcome.

I take a seat on the wooden bench and wait, watching the minutes pass on my phone screen and regretting not insisting I have a place inside the courtroom.

Finally, after an eternity, the doors fly open, and Travis exits with his sharply dressed lawyer, who pats him on the back and beams.

"As much as I enjoy working with you, Travis, I hope I don't have to see you anytime soon."

Travis laughs. "Me too. Thanks for everything."

"Call me if you need anything."

"Good news?" I ask Travis as his attorney walks way.

He nods and pulls me into his arms, not caring that there are plenty of other people wandering around us.

"You're with a free man," he declares, then considers me with pursed lips. "Well, a *taken* free man."

I can't help but grin like an idiot and kiss him.

"It feels a little surreal to be this happy," I admit once we break.

"Hold that thought." He pulls his notebook out of his pants pocket and jots that line down.

"You know, if you're going to start turning my words into lyrics, I'm at least going to expect a writer credit," I tease.

"I'll give you whatever you want." Travis chuckles. "I'll tattoo your name on my chest if it makes you happy."

"Don't go to extremes just yet," I say lightly. "We still have a European tour to get through, after all."

"Hey," a familiar voice catches our attention.

I tense up as my eyes land on Devin, who looks a little nervous to approach us.

"I just wanted to see you before I head out," he says.

Travis doesn't greet him like he used to, with open trust and love, but he's not entirely dismissive. "Thanks for coming today."

Devin nods as he slides his hands into his pockets. "I've been doing a lot of thinking and soul-searching, as fucking lame as that sounds, and I was hoping we could have dinner or something when you get back from the next leg of the tour?"

"Sure," Travis nods, holding out a fist for his brother to bump.

"Okay." Devin sounds relieved as his knuckles knock Travis's. "Good to see you, Dakota."

I offer a tight smile before he retreats.

"He wanted to testify on my behalf," Travis says quietly. "Not the most logical thing, really, but I appreciated the gesture. And it was an unnecessary one, given that the judge didn't even want to look at the progress notes from my therapist or letters from friends and the label advocating for me."

I frown. "Well, I'm just glad it's over."

"Me too. Especially because there's something I want to show you."

He holds my hand tightly in his as we head outside, where a few local photographers are staked out.

Ignoring them, he walks me to the passenger side of his low sports car, shielding me from the lenses of the photographers as I slide in, then shuts the door for me.

"Want to tell me where we're headed?" I ask when he's settled into the driver's seat.

"Home," he answers simply.

I squeeze his hand, content to be connected at the fingertips as he accelerates away from the courthouse.

It takes us twenty minutes of windy back roads before we turn down a paved, somewhat residential street.

"I would have thought you moved downtown," I say. "Lived in some new condo or something."

"I have a condo in Los Angeles, actually. But I've been thinking about putting it on the market."

"Done with the West Coast?" I prompt.

He shrugs. "Maybe."

That is one of the thousand things we need to decide on if this all works out.

Leigh, as promised, worked overnight to get the termination papers between the label and *Exos* finalized, and Dan already turned over all the footage to her directly.

After that, *Exos* released a statement, announcing my departure from the company, which was strange to be part of the news instead of reporting on it.

I expected some backlash, given my recent appearance in the gossip news, but I've already had three publications reach out and ask if I'm interested in freelance work or if I'm looking for a permanent position. Two of the jobs are in New York, and one's in D.C., but my future still seems to be firmly on the East Coast.

I start to imagine a life where I write from my tiny kitchen in Manhattan as Travis scribbles lyrics in his notebook—when we're not touring, of course—and I can't stop myself from falling in love with that unknown of seeing the world with him and creating a living on our own terms.

It's exhilarating, really, for a girl like me who once lived and breathed routine to be ecstatic about a lack of it.

"This is it," Travis says, sounding a little nervous as he pulls up to a gate and punches the button to open it.

I can only gape at the house that appears before me, tucked behind massive trees that already sport the orange-red hues of autumn. It's bigger than anything I ever dreamed of living in, and it's the perfect blend of modern and old Tudor styles, with a high-pitched roof and massive floor-to-ceiling windows.

I'm speechless as we step inside.

"There's not a lot of furniture...or anything else," he says, shifting his weight on his feet. "But I spent so much time over these past few years working on my mental space that I didn't really give a lot of attention to the physical one."

"You're being too hard on yourself," I tell him. "This is beautiful."

He exhales in relief. "I'm glad you like it."

I run my fingertips along the wrought iron banister as he leads me upstairs.

I figure he wants to give me a proper tour, maybe show me his bedroom, but instead, he pivots at the top of the stairs and leads me to a room that seems to be a catch-all for the variety of items his record label has sent him over the years.

It's like the equivalent of that bottom drawer at my desk in the *Exos* newsroom but way better and more substantial.

Plaques of gold-plated records lean against the wall, and

I eye a bag of what appears to be half-opened fan mail in the corner, but Travis opens the closet and pulls out a few plastic storage containers.

"Decided now's a good time to unpack?" I joke as he pops the lid.

He smiles but says nothing as he rummages through the boxes of notebooks.

Then it dawns on me.

These simple, ten-dollar bins house *thousands* of thoughts from Travis's mind over the years, and I immediately want to go through every single one of them.

I patiently wait for him to find what he's looking for, and a few minutes later, he pulls out a large composition notebook with a familiar black and white cracked marble pattern on the front.

"That looks like the notebook we used in English class," I say with a frown.

"That's because it is," Travis says lightly as he flips through some of the back pages. "Here."

I blink as I take in my own messy scrawl—there's a reason I write exclusively on phones and computers, after all—boldly filling out the peer review prompt at the end of the journal.

Then I read my past words aloud.

"'A little self-deprecating, a little cliché, but overall, beautifully vulnerable with a bit of honest chaos.'" I stop. "Travis. *Honest chaos?*"

"I lied to you before," Travis confesses, shoving his hands in his pockets. "Of course I remember you. How could I not? Even in the haze of smoke and how often I didn't attend class, I could see how determined you were.

264

You were always winning awards at our assemblies and stirring up shit with the student newspaper."

I clutch the notebook to my chest and reflect that it's an interesting part of the human condition, not knowing what actions we've taken that stand out to other people, leaving a lasting impression—that we may not even remember.

"It was big news when you won that scholarship," he continues, "and I was so damn jealous that you got a ticket out of town and I didn't. I can't honestly say I've carried a torch for you all these years, but I didn't outright dismiss the idea of asking you to write the piece when Leigh suggested it. I truly didn't think you'd take it, and when you did, I was a little pissed off at how you'd become everything I'd expected you to be, and more, defying my expectations with your tenacity and honesty and very sparing vulnerability."

I swallow. "And now?"

"And it's funny how a woman who skyrocketed to the top of her career at such a young age would even entertain the idea of being with someone like me," Travis says with certainty. "I'm just glad you said yes because, Dakota, my life is so much better with you in it."

"How are you so sure of this?" I ask. "I mean, we've barely scratched the surface of what it would even be like to be together."

He reaches into his pocket, pulling out his notebook and flipping to the page he's looking for, then hands it over.

"I wrote this the night we stayed up to midnight together," he says quietly. "I knew it then, and my feelings haven't wavered for a single second."

So desperately, fanatically, unbelievably in love with Dakota Shaw at midnight.

I laugh as the tears form in my eyes, and I slide the pen out of its little holster on the cover, writing my own declaration before I hand it back over to him.

I'm so madly in love with Travis Young at all times.

He grins at my words, and as we fall into each other's arms, there are no words left to say, write, or sing—just the promise of all the possibilities that lie together for us ahead.

EPILOGUE

THREE YEARS LATER

The internet in our house is shockingly reliable this morning.

We specifically chose to buy this place because of its remote location, but there have, thankfully, been sparingly few times it's been a little inconvenient to be disconnected from modern amenities.

It was by happenstance that we found this town, but for now, it's home.

After Travis's contractual obligations ended with the final performance of "Honest Chaos" in Berlin, we went on a little European tour of our own.

Just like we did in Seattle, we took our time sightseeing and traveling through every country Travis had visited but never got a chance to really *see*.

But when our rental car broke down in the middle of nowhere outside of Madrid, we walked past hills of olive trees and stumbled across this little wooden one-bedroom cabin.

It took a few months to make it ours, but now, we split our time between here, Travis's house in Pittsburgh, Phoenix and Nick's condo in New York, and whatever places we settle in when we have to be in a different city for a little while.

With my freelance work, I'm free to roam the globe as I choose, and I get a steady pay of royalties from the tell-all book on Ellison Incorporated I wrote between figuring out the visa situation and logistics of us emigrating from the U.S. to Spain.

If I could go back and do it all over again, I'd choose Travis and this life with him every single time.

And judging by the fact his new album has some pretty significant references to me, our conversations, and our relationship, I think he feels confident in his decision, too.

"You're up early," Travis says, smirking as he drops down beside me on our tiny but well-loved front porch. "Any particular reason?"

I exhale and lean into him, propping up my laptop on my knees. "Do you really not want to watch?"

He shrugs. "Leigh's been texting me updates."

After Travis officially went out on his own to form an independent label, he took Leigh, Phoenix, and Nick with him.

Although Travis put out his latest album as a solo artist, he signed Phoenix and Nick as his first—and only—talent, giving them the grace and means to continue the work on their second LP as a duo. They eventually worked out their issues, relationship-wise and as bandmates, and our last trip to New York was to celebrate their engagement and official public coming out.

My phone pings with a message from Leigh, telling me it's time.

Travis sighs as the intro music for the presenter comes on.

"Come on," I chide him. "You can admit you want to win this."

We sit, watching the slightly pixelated montage of all the artists and their videos, but Travis is the only one who isn't actually present in the theater. The camera pans to Nick and Phoenix who will accept the award on Travis's behalf if he wins.

Olivia O, an ultra-successful independent artist of her own right, holds up the envelope. "And the Grammy goes to..." She fumbles opening it slightly, and the audience laughs as she smiles. "'Forever Young at Midnight,' Travis Young."

The roaring of applause is clear, even through my laptop speakers, and our phones start buzzing with texts from Devin, Leigh, our parents, and other friends, but Travis still shakes his head, evidently nonplussed by the result.

"You're a Grammy-winning musician," I say proudly. "Congratulations, my love."

But it's not until he reaches over and picks up my left hand, bringing it to his mouth to place a kiss on my wedding ring, that he finally smiles.

BOOKS BY JENNIFER ANN SHORE

Young Adult Romances

Everywhere, Always

Just Play Pretend

Only You in Everything

Perfect Little Flaws

The Extended Summer of Anna and Jeremy

The Stillness Before the Start

Adult Romances

In the Now

Nothing Personal for Breakfast

This Is Your Life

Young at Midnight

"The Islands of Anarchy" Series

New Wave

Rip Current

"The Royally Human Vampire" Series

Metallic Red

Yes, Your Majesty

FREE GIFT FOR YOU!

Want to make your book an autographed copy? Head over to Jennifer's website and get a free bookplate!

https://www.jenniferannshore.com/bookplate

CONNECT WITH JENNIFER

Hi there,

I cannot thank you enough for reading my work. Truly, it means the world to me!

I'd love to connect with you on social media if you're up for it. I'm on all the major social channels, including TikTok (@jenniferannshore) and Instagram (@shorely).

And don't forget to subscribe to my email newsletter (jenniferannshore.com/newsletter) for bonus scenes, new release announcements, giveaways, and more.

All my love! —Jennifer

ACKNOWLEDGMENTS

I'm continually blown away by all of the pictures, texts, emails, and other means of communication people use to check in, promote my books, and say nice things. I can't thank everyone who reads/shares/supports my books and my work enough! THANK YOU.

Jen McDonnell, I don't know what I would do without all of your editing wizardry and you personally. Your brain is a godsend for my writing and my general sanity. JB and I love you!

Denise Leora Madre, there are hardly words to express how much your edits and suggestions mean to me. Thank you for being you and making me giggle like a maniac!

Lindsay Hallowell, thank you for all your patience with my stupid little errors and continual misuse of the same things always and adding extra words. I wish I could send you millions of macarons!

Kelly Lipovich, your talent is unmatched, and I'm so ridiculously happy that you share it with me (and my books and readers). Thank you for designing yet another perfect and beautiful cover.

Emily Wright, thank you for being my final sanity check and for all of your words of encouragement and cute dog pictures!

To my friends, family, my best friend/book photographer, and my husband—I'm beyond thankful for each and every single one of you.

To all my beta readers and ARC reviewers, thank you so much for amplifying my work and being so vocal in your support for my characters and books.

And for all of my lovely Instagram followers who voted in the best Tootsie Roll Pop flavor poll...I still think chocolate wins!

ABOUT THE AUTHOR

Jennifer Ann Shore is an award-winning, bestselling author based in Seattle, Washington.

She writes romance stories that go a little deeper than the standard tropes. Her lineup of more than a dozen books includes standalones, a dystopian series, and a vampire series—with titles such as "Perfect Little Flaws," "Young at Midnight," and "Metallic Red."

Prior to publishing, she led an impressive career in New York, first as a journalist and then as a marketing executive, gaining recognition for her work from companies such as Hearst and SIIA.

Be sure to sign up for her newsletter on her website (https://www.jenniferannshore.com) and follow her on Twitter (@JenniferAShore), Instagram (@shorely), and TikTok (@jenniferannshore).

Made in the USA
Middletown, DE
28 April 2022